The Giveaway Girl

Rose Marie Lambert DeHart

iUniverse, Inc.
Bloomington

The Giveaway Girl

iUniverse books may be ordered through booksellers or by contacting:

iUniverse
1663 Liberty Drive
Bloomington, IN 47403
www.iuniverse.com
1-800-Authors (1-800-288-4677)

ISBN: 978-1-4502-8556-8 (sc)
ISBN: 978-1-4502-8557-5 (ebook)

Printed in the United States of America

iUniverse rev. date: 3/22/2011

The Giveaway Girl is dedicated to my husband,
The Reverend Murry L. DeHart, Jr.,
and to our friend, Veronica,
who assisted me in editing this novel.

Chapter 1

She walked across the crowded fast food restaurant and precariously balanced a well-filled tray as she juggled a purse, cell phone, and numerous bags slung over her arms. She spied a small table occupied by a young man sitting alone. She approached the table.

"Do you mind? May I share your table?" she asked.

The young man looked up, smiled, and nodded yes, as he slightly arose, in acknowledgement of her presence. He touched the paper napkin to his lips.

"Of course, may I help?" he replied.

"No prob, I've got it all under control," she said as the contents of her purse tumbled to the tiled floor.

The young man reached down, scooped up the comb, lipstick, eyebrow pencil, tissues, et cetera, and very carefully returned them to the purse. He set the purse on the table and sat back down on the softly padded metal chair.

"I'm Scarlet," she said.

"I'm Ashley Wilkes." His eyes twinkled as he introduced himself.

"You must be joking."

"No, I'm afraid not. Mother is a big fan of *Gone With The Wind*, as you may have guessed. She even named our house Tara, although it is very modest in size, not at all like the Hollywood version." He paused. "I'm called Ash, but I couldn't resist giving you the full treatment," he added.

Ash looked on in astonishment as Scarlet organized the food on her tray. The tray contained a paper cup of water, a large pile of artificial sweetener and lemon packets, a burger on a bun, and packets of mustard, catsup, and pickle relish. She emptied two packets each of sweetener and lemon into the cup of water and stirred it with the plastic spoon.

As she concentrated on dressing the burger from the packets of mustard, catsup, and pickle relish, he observed that she was quite attractive. She wore her blonde hair in a stylish, shoulder length cut. He noted her petite figure was trim and well toned. The blue dress hugged her curves and deepened the blue of her eyes—the bluest he had ever seen. When she raised the burger to her lips, he noted her recently manicured nails. She wore conservative makeup.

Soon she was eating the burger and seemed to relish each bite. As she bent into the burger, the somewhat loose neckline of her dress slightly revealed nicely rounded breasts. He quickly looked away as she raised her eyes to meet his. Just at that moment, a dollop of mustard fell on the skin revealed in the open neckline. She quickly moved to mop it up with her paper napkin.

"Do you come here often?" Her mischievous grin was apparent as she uttered the age-old opening line and took a bite of the burger.

"Actually, no, I don't come here often. I met with a new client nearby and decided on a quick bite. It's somewhat off my beaten path. You?"

"What?"

"Do you come here often?"

She took a big gulp of the lemonade that she had made from the cup of water, pink packets, and lemon and shook her head indicating that she did not.

"I'm not from around here." She was hungrily chewing the burger.

"I came on Monday—what's today? Oh, I've been here a couple of days. Hadn't really planned to stay, but here I am."

Ash was obviously puzzled over this revelation, but continued eating his Happy Meal.

"Hey, is that a kid's meal? I didn't know grown-ups could order those. What will you do with the toy?" she asked.

"I have quite a collection of them for my sisters' kids. They love to see Uncle Ash arrive with his toy bag."

"That's a neat idea."

She continued eating the burger and licking her fingers.

Ash finished eating, wiped his mouth, cleaned the table in front of him, picked up all the scraps and dirty napkins, and placed them on his tray.

"Wow, you're neat. Bet your wife appreciates that," Scarlet commented.

"Oh, yes, by all means she appreciates my habits." He stood up, excused himself, and approached the trash bin near the door.

"Have a nice day," she called out.

"Thanks, you too," he responded. He looked back at the girl, as he pushed the door open, and made his way to the Hummer parked just outside the restaurant.

She watched as he moved his long legs into the Hummer. He was quite tall—tall enough to have played basketball in school. He was clean-shaved. His black hair, peppered with just enough gray to be interesting, was professionally styled.

He climbed in and placed the toy in a basket in the rear seat. As he reached to start the engine, he saw that she was still sitting inside the restaurant. For reasons he did not understand he felt that something was wrong and did not immediately move the Hummer.

He watched as she finished eating her meal, emptied the contents of the tray into the trash bin, made a trip to the restroom, and exited the door near his vehicle.

"Are you all right?" Ash opened the window and asked.

"Oh, yes I'm fine. Thanks for asking. I'm OK. I could use a ride though."

"I'm going past the Green Leaf Mall. Is that in your direction?"

"Yes, great. I need to get to the interstate."

He reached across the seat and opened the door as she crossed in front of the Hummer. She opened the rear door and tossed the bags, (he noticed there were two, the eco-friendly ones that some of the stores were giving away) into the rear seat. She quickly released her hold on the cell phone, dropped it into her purse, climbed in, fastened the seat belt, and settled into the seat.

"This is great. I really appreciate the ride."

"Do you have relatives here?" Ash inquired.

"Actually, I'm just passing through. Looks like a nice little town, though. Have you been here long?"

"North Carolina born and bred—lived here in Royal all my life, except college. I followed my Dad's example and graduated from Wake Forest University. My folks thought it would be a better experience to go away to school instead of Royal College and living at home."

"What line of work are you in?" Scarlet observed his well-tailored business suit, crisp white shirt, necktie, and matching pocket square. She assumed he was a professional.

"You mean you can't tell? I'm a CPA. Have my own firm with a small office force of accounting personnel."

"I noticed how neat and careful you were with your napkins and stuff." She dug into the large purse, pulled out an iPod, plugged it in to her ear, and settled back to listen.

Ash drove along in silence. He tried to explain to himself the uneasy feeling he had about this girl.

Suddenly she pulled the iPod from her ear and said, "Ash, I haven't been honest with you."

"Oh, are you an escaped criminal, maybe an ax murderer?" Ash asked, hoping to ease her into an explanation.

"No, it's nothing like that. It's just—well, I'm actually here on a mission."

"You're on a mission." It was a statement, not a question.

"Yes, I'm trying to find my father."

"I've lived here all my life, perhaps I know him. What's his name?"

"I don't know."

She paused to allow her statement time to register before continuing. "I'm not sure he lives here. It's very complicated. I just need a ride out to the interstate."

"Good, I'm headed in that direction. We'll be there in about ten minutes. Will that be convenient for you? If you need a bus, there's a stop there, too."

"That's great."

They rode on in silence.

When they passed a small campus, she asked, "Is that Royal College? It looks nice. I didn't get to college. I finished high school and took some courses in design at the community college. My folks were planning for me to go to college, but I had other things to do—better things than getting an education."

He detected the irony in her voice, but did not respond. They drove on in silence until he turned onto the interstate that would take him to the exit for the Green Leaf Mall.

"Where does the name Royal come from?" she asked.

"It's the name of the prominent family here. They are the founders of the town. They made their fortune in the hosiery mills until the outsourcing of jobs overseas nearly ruined the economy. The mills employed almost everyone in town and when the mills closed, the unemployment soared. However, Simon Royal came to the rescue when he came up with the Royal Winery."

"A winery supports this town? It must be some winery!"

"People jumped on the band wagon. This is grape country—been raising grapes for years for another company, so Simon just had to talk the folks into selling the grapes to him instead of the big guys.

"Then, they had to have barrels, so Simon, Junior started building barrels. More recently, they got into making apple cider. Growing apples and building barrels for the cider making is a big boon for our economy. We just do not have an unemployment problem. Simon, Junior discovered there was a shortage of barrels in the industry in other places as well. He supplies barrels for wineries all over the world."

"I guess the mall came next and all kinds of new business?"

Ash nodded his agreement. "My dad was treasurer of Royal Enterprises up until his death," he added.

"I guess that's why you're a CPA? Did you ever work for the Royals?"

"No, my dad's legacy to me was to set me up in my own accounting firm." Ash did not understand why he was telling her so much about his life.

He gave a turn signal, left the interstate, drove onto the access road, and pulled in front of the bus stop sign.

He turned to his passenger and asked, "Are you sure you're OK? I could help if you need it."

"Thanks, I'll just get my stuff out of the rear seat. Don't bother—the traffic is pretty heavy."

She opened the door, stepped from the Hummer, pulled her bags from the rear seat, and placed them on the curb. She stepped back and waved for him to drive on.

Chapter 2

*A*s he made his way back to the interstate, his thoughts remained on the young girl he had dropped off on the side of the road. He drove on in silence for a short distance. Suddenly, he picked up his cell phone and made a call to his office.

"Hi, Marlene, it's me, Ash." He spoke to the answering machine and realized that his secretary had not returned from lunch. He continued, "I'm running a little late. I should be there within the hour." He switched the cell phone off and made a quick exit.

His thoughts raced as he sped back to the bus stop. What was he thinking to leave a young woman, a girl really, alone at the bus stop in a strange town? His eyes searched the area around the bus stop before he actually reached it. The bus approached as he drew near. She was not catching this bus— she was nowhere in sight. There was no one in the area. He drove around the area and looked for her before he gave up and returned to his office.

Ash went into the break room and poured himself a cup of freshly brewed coffee. He returned to his office to think over the events of his lunch break. He leaned back in the leather-upholstered chair, sipped his coffee, and peered through the window.

He bought the house he grew up in near downtown Royal

and remodeled it for an office. The widening of the street left a small yard of lush green grass. The boxwoods his mother planted were now up to the windowsills and, he noted, in need of pruning.

His private office was, at one time, the dining room for the family. He removed the old French doors and replaced them with paneled doors to provide privacy. He held fond memories of Sunday dinners in this room. Dad carved the roast, or on holidays, turkey, and piled the slices on individual plates to be passed around the table. He was eleven and his sister Lorraine was sixteen when they moved into the larger house that his dad built on the hill, overlooking Royal Village—the original name of the town.

He reflected on growing up in the small town. The old post office was in the next block a short distance down the street. The bank was across the street. The library and newspaper office were nearby.

The newspaper office had been one of his favorite places. He loved the old time presses, the smell of ink, and the rush as the few employees hurried to get the newspaper out on time. Of course, computers do everything now, but in those days, he watched as Mr. Lambert typeset the daily newspaper on the Linotype.

As a boy, he thought he wanted to be a reporter or editor of the paper. He made up stories and wrote imaginary accounts of local events. These journals were stored in a closet in the old dining room that he called 'my office'.

Ash sipped the last of his coffee. His thoughts returned to the young girl he had dropped off at the bus stop. How could he have done such a thing? He would leave work early, return to the mall, and look for her. Scarlet—he had never met anyone named Scarlet.

Chapter 3

*A*s usual, Ash was unable to leave the office on time. He was in the middle of the final rush as busy workers made the effort to get home in time for dinner. He drove straight to the bus stop where he had left Scarlet, but she was, of course, nowhere around. He circled the mall and its parking deck, but there was no sign of her. He parked the Hummer as near to the entrance as possible. He entered the lower level, and walked slowly around the mall.

He realized that he had not been here in months. How long had it actually been? Some of the regular shops had closed and new places were open but he noted there were still many empty stores on this level. He didn't remember there being so many kiosks where jewelry, flowers, and other small items were for sale. He walked to the escalator and took the treads two at a time until he reached the second level.

He stopped long enough to check his cell phone and read from a list he had been making for several days. He had waited for a day when he could take the time to shop. He saw he needed mouthwash, dental floss, and vitamins, all of which he could purchase in one stop. He walked toward the drugstore that anchored one end of the mall.

Ash remembered when Marlene first started working for him, she offered to take care of his shopping, but he refused. She seemed eager to do personal errands for him, but he always avoided her offers. His friends told him she had an ulterior motive. He was never sure of this idea, but continued to shop for himself and had not regretted his decision.

Ash entered the drugstore and looked around for the items he needed. He ended up at the magazine stand where he picked up the latest issue of one of his favorite periodicals. He stopped at the cash register on the way out and paid for his purchases.

He left the store, stepped on the escalator, descended toward the lower level, and spied Scarlet. He hurriedly exited the escalator and ran toward her. Just as he called out, she entered the restroom. He sat on a bench in sight of the restroom and tried not to be obvious.

It seemed an interminable amount of time before she re-appeared and immediately saw Ash. She hesitated as if she did not know whether to approach him or not. When he stood up, she called to him.

"Hi, Ash! What brings you to the mall?"

"I needed to pick up a few things," he said, waving the bag he held. "Truth be told, I was looking for you. I worried about putting you out at the bus stop. Did you miss the bus? Is everything OK?" He noticed she only carried her purse. The other bags were nowhere in sight.

"Sure, why wouldn't it be?" She ignored his first question.

"I have this feeling that something is wrong. Could I be of help?"

"Gee, that's kind of you. Really, I'm fine."

"Have you had dinner? It's still early. I'm starved and would enjoy having some company."

"As a matter of fact, I haven't eaten since that fast food lunch. I would love to have dinner with you. That is if your wife wouldn't mind?"

"My wife? I don't understand."

"You know—I commented that your wife must appreciate you. You replied that she did. You know, cleaning up the napkins and stuff."

"Oh that! I'm not married. It just didn't seem necessary to explain. I was leaving and I thought that was the end of it," Ash explained. "Now that we have taken care of my marital situation—I know a good restaurant off the interstate. Shall we?" He pointed to the exit and they went out to the Hummer.

He opened the door, assisted her into the front seat, closed the door, and walked around to the driver's side. He entered the vehicle and started the engine. Soon he headed toward the area just off the interstate where the well-known chain restaurants were located.

He looked at the profile of the young girl sitting beside him and realized that his first appraisal of her was correct. She was young, very beautiful, and sexually attractive.

He looked again and noted that she had done something different with her hair—pulled it back and fastened it with a large silver barrette.

"How does a nice thick steak sound?" he asked.

"That sounds great! I'm sure you're hungry—a Happy Meal isn't very filling."

"You're right about that," Ash replied.

"I've been wondering—do you have relatives here?" Ash inquired.

"No," she replied with no other comment.

"I didn't mean to pry."

"It's OK. I'll only be here a day or so. I have a lead on someone who may be helpful in finding my father."

"If I can help in any way, just let me know," Ash offered. He concentrated on the traffic and remained quiet.

In a short time, they arrived at the restaurant, parked, and exited the vehicle. The restaurant nestled among the well-known chain restaurants. Its elegant simplicity was a relief from the garish, flashing neon of its neighbors. Scarlet noticed there was no sign giving its name.

She hopped out without waiting for him to open the door. However, he managed to reach the restaurant door first. He held it open for her as she walked through. The thought crossed his mind that Francine would never open a door for herself, if Ash were available to open it for her. He liked opening doors—his father had taught him what he considered proper behavior for a gentleman.

The hostess greeted him. "Good evening, Mr. Wilkes. It is so good to see you. May I show you to your regular table?"

"Yes, thank you, Yvonne."

He followed Scarlet as Yvonne showed them to a table near the French doors that led to a patio. He held the chair for Scarlet and took a seat on the opposite side of the table, facing the patio. Ash observed that there were several diners this evening.

The décor of the restaurant was reminiscent of Colonial Williamsburg. Two traditional chairs upholstered in blue velvet flanked the fireplace. Swags at the window were made of a linen fabric hand embroidered with butterflies and flowers. A Persian rug defined the space in front of the fireplace. Brass wall sconces provided the soft lighting. Music was playing in the background.

Scarlet looked at her surroundings. "I'm always interested in décor. This is lovely. I have a design business. I design store windows."

"That sounds like a good business. It must be fulfilling to look back and see what you have created."

"Yes, it's nice to do something I love. And, fortunately, it pays the bills, too," she replied.

Scarlet picked up the menu. After reading over the selections, she asked Ash to order for her. When the waiter appeared, Ash called him by name and ordered prime rib for two and a bottle of the best Royal wine.

"Well," Ash began, "did you have a pleasant day? We are proud of our new mall. It has nice shops for such a small town. It's a good place to shop."

"I didn't do any shopping."

Ash was extremely curious about her presence in town. He

was trying discreetly, he hoped, to learn more about this young woman.

"I went to the library," she added.

"The library? That's quite a distance from the mall."

"Yes, I thumbed a ride with a nice old man in a pickup truck."

"Grizzly beard? Old faded red pickup?"

"Yes, he said his name was Doc Hadley."

"That was Doc, all right. He's safe enough, just a little balmy at times. Probably you were in more danger from his driving than anything else."

"He was OK. He drove too slow. That was the danger."

"Doc was a collector of vintage cars, especially old race cars. He had quite a collection at one time. I think he raced back in his younger days—nothing big time, small local races." Ash paused and continued. "Even here in Royal, there are some dangerous characters. You shouldn't hitch rides. Of course, it's none of my business."

"That's right."

"Excuse me?"

"I agree—it's none of your business." Scarlet re-considered her sassy remark and added, "I suppose I don't want to be treated like a child. Will you forgive me?" She smiled at him in an attempt to remedy the situation.

"Of course, there's nothing to forgive. Perhaps I overstepped my bounds," Ash replied.

They sat quietly until the salads arrived. The waiter offered several choices of dressings. They ate the salads with very little conversation.

When the prime rib arrived, Scarlet showed her delight. She dazzled Ash with her smile and poked the steak with her fork.

She exclaimed, "Wow, that's beautiful. It's cooked just right."

Ash smiled at her enthusiasm. She was so fresh and so lovely. Conversation suddenly resumed.

"I really am enjoying our meal together. This is an elegant place. Thank you so much." Scarlet expressed appreciation.

"You're very welcome. I'm enjoying your company." Ash was pleased to realize the mood was, once again, lighter following his expression of concern for Scarlet.

When the prime rib was a succulent memory, they selected two chocolate filled raspberry tarts from the dessert tray, offered by the waiter.

The maitre d' came to the table as they finished dessert. He said, "It's good to see you, Mr. Wilkes. Come again soon." Ash responded with a smile and a nod and they arose and left the restaurant.

When they reached the Hummer, Scarlet said, "I'm sorry to be so nosy, but you didn't pay for our meal."

"That's OK. I know the owner." Ash smiled as he opened the door of the Hummer.

"You know the owner?"

"Yes, it's one of my new investments. We've only been open a short time and are doing very well. It's the first fine dining place in Royal City and it's hugely successful. The chef trained at a culinary school in New England. I have a sommelier coming on board next month. He is currently training in New England, as well. That's when we join the big time!"

As Ash guided her into the Hummer, Scarlet asked, "Sommelier? That's something to do with wine, isn't it?"

"Yes, he's a wine specialist. We already have a wine cellar and he will be in charge of ordering and stocking it. He will be knowledgeable and capable of assisting the diners in selecting wines compatible with their choice of entrée." Ash explained.

"I'm impressed—very metropolitan."

As soon as Scarlet was seated, Ash moved into the drivers' seat, left the parking lot and headed back toward Royal.

"I noticed, earlier, you said Royal City. Is that a prediction?" she asked.

"I didn't realize I said that. I'm on the Royal Town Council and, yes, we hope to get the name changed in the near future. We're already reaching fame in the wine industry."

Ash drove along slowly. "Where are you staying—so I can drop you off," he inquired.

"Oh, just take me back to the mall. I'll catch a bus from there."

"Sorry, Miss Scarlet, this little town doesn't have a local bus after six o'clock."

"Just take me to the mall and I'll get a cab. I really don't want to put you to any trouble."

"No trouble at all. This town is small so it can't be very far."

"I'll be fine. Just let me out at the mall." She emphasized this statement—Ash knew she was serious. He reluctantly drove to the mall and chose a spot that was particularly bright with outside lights.

"I don't like this," he said.

"Please, I'm staying near the mall. Just unlock the door, please."

"This isn't right. I don't want to leave you here. The mall is closed. There's no one around."

"Thanks for a lovely evening. Goodbye." She quickly unlocked the door and left the vehicle.

It was difficult getting through the closing time traffic. By the time Ash was able to park the Hummer and jump out, she had disappeared. He walked around the area and did not see any sign of her. He returned to the vehicle and circled the parking lot. He did not see her—it was as though she had vanished. There was something strange going on. He drove across town to his condominium.

Chapter 4

$\mathcal{A}$sh lived in a luxury condominium converted from an old school building that had housed all grades, one through twelve. The developer of the property renovated, modernized, and turned it into upscale living spaces for the wealthy citizens of Royal. Ash was one of the first to buy. He entered the elevator for the ascent to his spacious home on the third floor of the building. It had housed his fifth grade classroom along with several other elementary grades. Ash had requested that the builder retain the original floors. He, the builder, had sanded and polished them to a beautiful, lustrous finish. Each time Ash stepped into this place, he wondered how many young feet had walked these boards.

When he bought the house, he employed a decorator, but shortly dismissed her because she insisted on furnishing the place with all glass and chrome. He was traditional, and with his mother's guidance, he had created a comfortable home. It reflected his good taste. He loved expensive furnishings and accessories. He enjoyed taking his time to find exactly the right pieces for every room.

The foyer was large and furnished in dark woods. The brass lamps reflected in the mirrors on opposite walls. Gold colored silk moiré covered the walls. A Persian rug in bold colors of black, red, and gold anchored the floor under the antique table. Original artwork adorned the table, and the wall above it.

The living room flowed smoothly from the foyer in similar pieces of antique furniture and Persian rugs in the same bold colors. His office/den held a custom made bookcase filled with his favorite volumes. Many first editions, held upright by large brass bookends, sat on the shelves. Additional brass artwork gleamed on the shelves. His massive hand carved desk was free of all clutter.

After a brief stop in the bathroom, he went into the kitchen. He opened the door of the large wall unit refrigerator, removed, and popped the top on a can of orange juice. He drank it quickly before going into the bedroom. He removed his business suit and very carefully placed it onto a wooden hanger. The hanger took its place in the perfectly arranged large walk in closet/ dressing room. The silk pajamas felt good against his skin as he returned to his bedroom. He sat down and tried to figure out what the story of Miss Scarlet could be. He suddenly realized that he did not know her last name.

He replayed the afternoon and evening in his mind, but still could not come to any conclusion about the mysterious young girl. After he glanced at the daily newspaper, he retired for the night, and began a fitful sleep. Normally he had no trouble sleeping, but this night was different.

Chapter 5

*A*sh arose early and had his usual bowl of cereal with fat free milk. After he showered and dressed, he left to attend to the business of the day.

As he left the parking garage, Ash once again reflected on the events of the previous day. Without realizing it, he found himself heading once again to the Green Leaf Mall. Why would he do such a thing? Surely, he did not expect to find Scarlet wandering around the mall at this early hour. He turned onto the access road that led to the mall and saw a traffic jam. He could see the flashing red light that meant there was an accident up ahead. He left the main road for one that turned into the back of the mall and began his circle of the stores. It was half past eight o'clock.

He continued his circuit around the perimeter of the mall. The stores were not open, although the entrances to the mall were unlocked. A group of senior citizens gathered for their morning walk around the lower court. Some said two times around the mall made a mile. They called themselves the Mall Milers.

He was not surprised that he did not see Scarlet as he turned the Hummer toward his office in downtown Royal. The sleepy little village grew more congested with traffic. Ash thought that it would not be long until the streets would need widening. He personally liked the small town atmosphere and did not look forward to the changes that he knew were coming. His friends were urging him to run for mayor. Perhaps it was time to consider putting his name on the ballot.

There was nothing of importance in the morning mail. He sat with his second cup of coffee and scanned reports that he had neglected the day before. Suddenly, Marlene appeared at his doorway. After a light tap on the half open door, she opened it and entered his office.

"Ash, I don't know what to make of this call. It's from the highway patrol and concerns someone named Scarlet."

"I'll take it. Put it through, please."

She rang and he immediately picked up.

"This is Ashley Wilkes."

"Scott Barnes, here. I'm with the North Carolina Highway Patrol. Sorry to bother you, but we have a young lady here who asked us to call you. She said she doesn't know anyone else in town."

"What is it?" asked Ash. He immediately thought of the flashing red lights at the mall.

"There's been an accident involving this young lady. She gave us your name and asked that we call you. She's in the Royal Hospital Emergency Room. Sorry to inconvenience you, but—"

"I'll be right there." He replaced the receiver and headed for the door.

"Marlene, I'll be back as quickly as possible."

He raced to the Hummer and was soon on his way across town to the small hospital his family had helped fund. He pulled into the parking lot near the emergency room, jumped out, and entered the emergency room area. A nurse, whom he recognized as a former high school classmate, ushered him to a curtained off cubicle where he saw the pale, white face of Scarlet. He saw immediately that she was unconscious.

The trooper greeted him with a handshake. He said, "I'm Sgt. Scott Barnes. A car struck her on the access road leading to the interstate. The drunk driver is in custody now. The young lady was alert in the beginning. She asked me to contact you, but she's out cold now. Do you know her?"

"I met her yesterday afternoon near the mall and gave her a lift. I don't know much about her—she seems to be just passing through town. She appears to be all alone."

"Is there anything else you can tell us?"

"I'm afraid not." Ash told the trooper about their meeting and the fact that he had seen her again at the mall and they had dinner together. "I'm sorry. I can't tell you anything else. I wish I could," Ash continued.

"I'll run a check on her and see if there is anything of note. She's pretty young—probably twenties."

"Have they examined her yet?"

"Yes, the nurse checked her vitals. Everything is functioning properly. She has a bump on her head from the accident. The doctor says that could have caused her to be unconscious."

Suddenly, Scarlet began to stir. She made a small noise. As her eyes opened, she looked around as if trying to recognize her surroundings.

Ash leaned over the railing of the emergency room bed. In a very hushed voice he said, "You're in the hospital. I'm Ash and I'm here to help."

"Thanks," she replied and drifted away again.

"Her name is Scarlet, but I'm afraid I don't know her last name. I'll stay here with her—at least until she regains consciousness."

The nurse came in. She looked at Ash and the trooper. "The emergency room doctor is on his way in. You may sit in the waiting room while he completes his examination," she instructed them.

Ash and the trooper stepped outside the emergency area. "So, you don't know anything about the young lady? Is that right?" Scott turned to Ash and inquired.

"Yes, that's it."

"I think she's of age so there's nothing to worry about there."

Ash was surprised at this remark. "Excuse me?"

"I understand—picking up a girl like that."

"Like what?"

"I see them coming through here all the time. We troopers practically have to beat them off. With us, it's the uniforms. That's what gets them!" He nudged Ash in the side and gave him a knowing look.

"Trust me, you have it all wrong. It wasn't what you think. We met at a fast food restaurant. I saw her again later and asked her to dinner. That's all it was." Ash was clearly annoyed at having to give an explanation to the trooper. He continued, "I was not present at the accident. I don't think we have anything else to say. Please excuse me."

He went back inside the hospital. After a short interval in the emergency room waiting area, he returned to the cubicle to find Scarlet awake. The doctor had been in.

"I'm pleased you had the nurse call me. We'll just wait and see what the doctor has to say about you. Get some rest and we'll talk later." He leaned over the bed railing and quietly reassured her.

"I'm not hurt. I just need to get out of here."

"Do you know what happened?" Ash asked.

"I'm trying to remember. I had breakfast at a place on the access road near the mall, local place, I think."

"Probably Minnie's?" Ash asked.

"Yes, I think so. The waitress was Dinah. She told me she had worked there since it opened. Has two grown sons she sent through school."

Ash knew Dinah—he had prepared her income tax returns for years and he knew all about her sons. Dinah's husband had left her alone when the boys were teens. She had managed to get enough grant money and financial aid to send them to college. They too, left her before the ink was dry on their diplomas, but to Scarlet he only said, "I know the place. And, I know Dinah."

"It was a good breakfast. I left there and started to cross the access road, and—sorry, the next thing I remember was the siren wailing."

The curtain parted and the emergency room doctor appeared. "I'm Dr. Rasheed. Are you a relative?" He aimed his question toward Ash.

"No, as a matter of fact I just met Scarlet yesterday afternoon. She's visiting our town and called me because she doesn't know anyone else here."

"I see. I have performed a preliminary examination of her vital signs. I see no problem there. However, we need to send her down for some ex-rays and perform some tests. She will need to stay overnight. She has a large contusion on her head. I would like her to stay for observation. We need someone to assume responsibility."

Scarlet spoke up, "I have insurance, but I don't know where my purse is."

The nurse, who had entered with the doctor, motioned to the shelf underneath the bed. She said, "Your purse is there." The nurse reached beneath the bed, retrieved the purse, and handed it to the patient. Scarlet removed the cards and handed them to the nurse.

"I'll have these scanned into the computer and we'll admit you from here. We'll get you into a room as soon as possible." She left the cubicle.

"You will see Dr. Fielding after you are admitted and transferred to a room. I wish you well." Dr. Rasheed left the cubicle.

"Ash, can you tell me what happened?"

"You were hit by a car near the access road at the mall. An ambulance brought you to the hospital. That's how you ended up here, in the emergency room."

"What about the driver?" asked Scarlet. Ash reached for her

hand—it felt cold to his touch. She slightly squeezed his hand and smiled up at him.

"They got the driver. He was still drunk from the night before."

"I heard someone say, just before I passed out, that he was 'driving under the influence.' So I suppose he was arrested."

"He's in lock up now. Fortunately, he stopped," Ash replied.

"I don't remember seeing him."

"That probably isn't unusual. I think nature has a way of protecting us in this type of situation." Ash spoke quietly. He continued, "While they are transferring you to a room, I need to go back to my office. I'll be back very soon. OK?"

"Of course, it's OK, but you don't need to bother with me. I'll be fine."

"Is there someone I could call? I would be happy to let your family know where you are."

"No, thanks, you've done enough. I'll wait for the tests and if I need to, I'll call Dad. Thank you for coming."

Ash knew instinctively that she did not intend to make a telephone call, but he did not comment. He started to the door, paused, and returned to her bedside.

"Call me if you need anything before I get back." He jotted his cell phone number on the back of his business card and handed it to her.

"Thanks. I'll probably be having x-rays and stuff. Just wait and come back after work. I'll be fine," Scarlet replied. She accepted the card and smiled at Ash as he left the room.

He drove straight to the office ready to resist the third degree from Marlene. He was determined not to tell her anything about his activities of the morning. He walked very quickly past her desk, with nothing but a nod. Of course, this did not stop Marlene—she followed him into his private office.

"I hope everything's all right?" she inquired.

"Everything's fine, thank you. I need to make a few phone

calls, please excuse me." He sat down at his desk and picked up the telephone. "Oh, and please close the door. Thank you." He could tell from the set of her shoulders that she objected to his dismissal, but he did not intend to tell her about his meeting with Miss Scarlet. Once again, he realized he did not know her last name.

Marlene returned to her desk, retrieved her cell phone from her purse, and made a call to Francine. She keyed in the number, all the while muttering to herself, "Francine thinks she is Ash's fiancée—that'll be the day!"

Chapter 6

At the end of the day, before he returned to the hospital, Ash went home and checked his mail. He received his personal mail at home, instead of at the office. When he first opened his office, he received all of his mail there, but soon realized that he wanted his personal life separate from his professional life. Marlene was a capable secretary, but he felt the need for a certain amount of privacy where his personal life was concerned. He preferred this arrangement. It had worked for him.

He changed into casual clothes. He decided he needed an apple to hold him over until he could get dinner. He chose one from the fruit bowl and returned to the hospital.

As he entered the front entrance to the hospital, he met the nurse who had attended Scarlet in the emergency room.

"Hi, I just went up to check on your friend. She seemed so alone. I went by for a minute. She's doing well. I think she just had a nasty bump on the head. She's a lucky girl. She's in 214." She spoke as she moved through the door and headed for the parking lot.

"Thanks," Ash called out, and proceeded to the elevator.

He tapped on the door. "Come in," Scarlet called out. He opened the door and looked around. Scarlet rested in bed— propped up on pillows, with a small bandage on her forehead.

"You are so kind to me. I really do appreciate you," she

spoke. She extended her hand. It was warm when he wrapped his hand around hers. He suddenly felt tenderness toward this girl that he barely knew.

"I realized this afternoon that I don't know your last name," he said.

"I was hoping you wouldn't ask! You probably won't believe it! It's O'Hara!"

"You're right! I don't believe it! What are the odds of Scarlet and Ashley getting together after all these years! My mother would absolutely love this!"

"O'Hara is my stepfather's name. He adopted me and he's the only father I ever knew."

"So, your search for your real father is the reason you're here? How's that going?"

"I'm not making any headway—not much I can do from this hospital bed. I mentioned to you that I had a lead in my father's identity. I had an appointment this morning. I hope I'll be able to set it up again."

"I'm available to help you any way I can. Just let me know." Ash was sincere in his offer, but reserved asking any questions. He thought she would confide in him when she was ready.

He settled himself into the recliner beside the bed.

"Have you seen the doctor? Any news?" he inquired.

"Dr. Rasheed sent me up here, but Dr. Fielding admitted me. He said the x-rays didn't show any problem. I should be able to leave in the morning. I'm feeling fine now and could probably leave, but they think I need to stay overnight."

"I'm sure that is a good idea—staying overnight." Ash paused and added, "Scarlet, you've been a mystery lady so far. I have no idea where you live or where you stay here in Royal. Don't you think it's time to 'fess up'?"

"I'm staying near the mall. Could we just leave it at that for now?"

"Yes, of course. I have no right to question you. Now, what can I do to make you more comfortable? Are you hungry?

Thirsty? Tell me what you need."

"You're such a dear. I'm fine. They brought me supper. I would already be out of your life if that car had not hit me. It came out of nowhere." She paused and continued, "I was going to call and thank you for the lovely dinner last evening. That's neat. You have your own restaurant. I didn't see a name anywhere, must be new?"

"I enjoyed it too. It was very pleasant. I haven't come up with a name yet. I think all of the customers refer to it as Ash's so that may be what I will end up calling it. I have always been interested in fine dining and wines. I decided to bring a little epicurean experience to Royal. I would like to take time off in the next year or so for some travel to the vineyards and wineries of France and Italy. I've read everything I could find about Tuscany. That's one of my travel goals."

"That sounds good. I would like to travel." Her voice was beginning to slur. Ash wondered if they had given her a sedative. He sat quietly for a while and when he saw that she was resting comfortably, he slipped away.

Chapter 7

*A*sh drove straight home and entered the secured parking garage in the lower level of the building. He took the elevator to the first floor, retrieved the evening newspaper, and bounded up the stairs to the top floor. He gave a hurried look at the mail and finding nothing of urgency went to the kitchen to forage in the refrigerator for food. He had to make do with a ham and cheese on wheat bread and a Diet Coke as he watched the evening news.

There was nothing new. They were still talking about the economy, the BP oil spill, and the weather. That was about it. His thoughts turned to Francine, the woman he had been seeing for a couple of years. This was a small town. Ash thought he should tell her of his recent adventure before she heard it from someone else. Even though there was no engagement, Ash wanted to be honest and above board about his recent activities.

Ash hit speed dial on his cell phone and waited for her to answer.

"Hello, Ash."

"Hello, hope you're OK this evening?"

"Yes, of course. And, you?"

"I've had something of an adventure."

"Tell me about this adventure. I didn't think anything adventurous happened in this town."

Perhaps she had not heard about his meeting with Scarlet. He proceeded to give her a shortened version of the last two days, omitting her unbelievable name and the dinner at his restaurant.

"My goodness, where is this young lady now?"

"She was taken by ambulance to the hospital. Poor kid, she doesn't know a soul in town. I went by the hospital after work and she's doing fine. When they release her in the morning, I'll give her a ride to the bus and she'll be on her way. Tell me about your day."

"Nothing exciting happened. I had lunch with a group of my colleagues. They want me to run for district judge. I don't think I'm interested, but I'm flattered that they thought of me."

"That sounds pretty exciting to me. You would be a terrific judge. You have my vote."

"I don't think I'll enter the race. My practice is about all I can handle right now, without hitting the campaign trail." There was a brief silence. She continued, "I'll see you over the weekend?" It was a question.

"Yes, of course. Call you tomorrow," Ash replied.

He turned off the cell phone, leaned back in the recliner, and was soon asleep. When he awoke the television set was still on. The news was the same—the economy and the oil spill. He pointed the remote, clicked off the set, changed into his pajamas, and retired for the evening.

Chapter 8

He slept well in spite of the events of the previous two days. After showering and dressing, he decided to raise his cholesterol, by having breakfast at Minnie's restaurant. Traffic was very mild at this early hour. He sped along the interstate until the billboard proclaiming Minnie's Best Pancakes pointed the way to the exit that led to the restaurant. Ash normally adhered to a strictly healthy diet, but this morning he intended to eat a big, country breakfast.

Dinah was behind the counter, blowing bubbles and cracking her chewing gum like a champion. Ash tried to hide his disgust at this annoying habit as he made his way to a booth. He picked up the menu and awaited Dinah's appearance at the booth with a mug of steaming coffee, already sugared and creamed just the way he liked it.

"Mornin', doll." She greeted Ash and placed the mug on the table.

"Good morning, Dinah. Hope you're well?"

"Yeah, I'm fine. Ain't heard from my tax refund yet. Whatta ya' think? Government gone broke?"

"Well, Dinah, I hate to be the one to bring you the bad news, but I sometimes wonder."

"What can I get you this morning? I hope it ain't poached eggs. How about a nice big breakfast? I'll bring you something to put some meat on your bones." She removed the pad from her back pocket, the pencil from the huge bun of dyed red hair and poised to take his order.

"Dinah, I'm going to make your day. Raise my cholesterol. Bring me The Big Killer."

"Now, let's don't do anything crazy! I don't want your death on my shoulders. I'm just kidding. The Big Killer won't hurt you every once in a while. I eat it every now and then and look at me—I'm skinny as a rail. Always have been. No matter what I eat."

"I'll have your breakfast out in a jiffy," she said

Ash picked up the newspaper from the table and looked at the headlines before checking the sports page. There isn't much going on this time of year. Dinah returned with his breakfast.

"Have you got a minute to talk, Dinah?"

"Sure, what do you want to talk about?"

"Do you remember talking to a young girl in here a day or so ago? Nice looking—"

Dinah interrupted, "You mean Scarlet?"

"Yes."

"Yeah, I remember. What do you want to know?"

"Anything you can tell me about her. A car hit her. She's in the hospital. No serious injuries, but she doesn't talk much. I would appreciate anything you can tell me about her."

Dinah moved into the seat opposite him.

"You know, I got the feeling that girl is in trouble. I think she's running from something or someone. There's a sad look about her. Let me see if I can remember anything that would help you." Dinah lit up a cigarette and blew the smoke out into the restaurant.

She said, "She didn't say much—it was more what she didn't say. I can't put my finger on it, but she is a very distressed little girl. She's not exactly a little girl—it just seems that way. How old do you think she is? I figure about twenty five, maybe thirty." She answered her own question. "I'm sorry I can't help you anymore than that, but she was in here at the busiest time

31

of the morning. She said she had an appointment in town."

"An appointment in town? I wonder who she was to see. Any idea?"

"I just don't remember, Ash. I'm sorry, but if she told me who she was meeting, I guess I forgot."

"That's OK, Dinah. If you remember anything else, please call me at this number." He added his cell phone number to one of his business cards and handed it to Dinah. She stuck it in the pocket on her uniform, left the booth, and turned her attention to other customers. Ash ate his breakfast in silence, paid the tab, and waved goodbye to Dinah as he left the restaurant. She returned his wave. She hurried to the table and picked up the generous tip she had come to expect from Ash.

He started toward the hospital, but decided to return home and exchange the Hummer for the Lexus. He thought perhaps Scarlet would be more comfortable in a sedan rather than the Hummer. She could have new aches and pains this morning. He would bring her to his home, if she would agree to it.

Ash used his card to open the underground garage. He parked the Hummer. As he moved his long legs out of the vehicle, he spied the Winslow sisters leaving in their chauffeur driven sedan. He waved at them and their car stopped.

Angela opened her window. "Good, morning, Ashley. We haven't seen you in several days. Hope all is well with you. How is your lovely mother?" she inquired.

"She's fine, Miss Angela. I talk to her on the telephone every day and try to visit every weekend."

"You're such a good boy! Blessings to you." She motioned for Miles to drive on. They headed for the weekly grocery run to the Piggly-Wiggly.

Through his friendship with the Winslow sisters, Angela and Isabella, Ash had learned that they were two of the most interesting residents of the building. Their ages were a heavily guarded secret, although many thought that Angela was the older of the two. They were both petite of build and had light brown hair misted with gray. They had trim, neat figures and were always fashionably dressed.

Their Papa, as the sisters referred to him, died many years ago and left them with a fortune whose origin was subject to speculation. Many people knew that he was a famous bootlegger during the days of prohibition. As children, they had lived in the mountains of North Carolina where bootlegging was a way of life. The souped up old cars that were used to outrun the revenue agents led the way to NASCAR racing and made many racing legends among the drivers.

As soon as their mother learned about Papa's illegal activities, she took her daughters and fled to the lowlands—where she was born. Papa provided them with a fine home, and an education. He stayed in the background for the most part.

Both young ladies, Isabella and Angela grew up in a home of wealth and refinement. Their introduction to society came at the state's Terpsichorean Debutante Ball. They became officially eligible for courting by the young bachelors of the county. However, neither of the ladies ever married. After their mother died, they were among the first residents of The Old School House bringing their longtime chauffeur with them.

Miles had been their chauffeur for many years. He remained with them when they left the large estate and moved into The Old School House. He had a small apartment—bedroom and sitting room—in their condominium. He was always available to chauffeur them. Neither of the ladies had learned to drive. The three became a small family, with Miles as the cook. It seemed to be a good arrangement for all three. They also employed a part-time housekeeper.

Ash waved at them and exited the garage himself. He was annoyed at being off his schedule. Eating breakfast at Minnie's had caused the delay. He checked in at the office and left without telling Marlene his destination—only that she could reach him on his cell phone, if necessary.

He headed to the hospital. He decided it would be a nice

surprise if he had flowers for Scarlet. He made a stop at the floral shop and bought a bouquet of mixed flowers.

When he entered the room that he had left the evening before, she was sitting in a chair dressed and ready to leave.

She spoke first. "Morning, it's good to be out of bed. I'm not a very good patient."

Ash handed her the flowers. "Oh, I doubt that. Most of us don't want to be in bed when we feel well. Did they discharge you? Are you ready to leave?" Ash inquired.

She smiled up at him and reached for the flowers. "Thank you, they are beautiful." She lifted the bouquet to her nose, sniffed, and continued speaking, "All of the paperwork is finished, and I'm ready to go. The nursing assistant will take me down in a wheel chair. You can bring the car to the main entrance. I'm sorry to be a bother to you. I need to see Dr. Fielding the first of the week. That is, if I'm still in town."

"A wheel chair?" Ash looked alarmed. He envisioned broken bones.

"It's just a hospital rule. They always escort departing patients."

"Good, then, I'll see you downstairs." Ash left the room. He brought the car around to the main entrance, where she waited in a wheel chair, accompanied by a nurse.

As soon as they were underway, she said, "I'm grateful for all you've done. I didn't intend to be a nuisance. You can just take me back to the mall and I'll get a bus from there." Ash saw that she still held the flowers in her hand. He was pleased that he had thought to surprise her.

"Scarlet, I'm just a bit outdone by you. I don't know anything about you. You always want to get out at the mall. Now, tell me what's up with you?"

"Please, trust me and let me out at the mall. You don't need to worry about me. I'll be fine."

"I'm sorry. I can't leave you at the mall or on the side of the road. You must let me help you. For now I'll take you to my house and later we'll decide what to do."

Neither of them spoke until they were in the elevator at The Old School House. "You'll be comfortable here today. You received quite a hit on your head. I'll feel better if you stay here and rest, in the event that you have a problem. I'll get you settled in and then go to the office. No need to protest. That's the way it is," he said.

He showed her around the condominium, making certain there was food in the refrigerator. After settling her in, he left for the office.

When he arrived, Marlene followed him into his office with a cup of coffee. She was bursting with curiosity, but did not question him.

As soon as he settled into the chair behind his desk, he said, "Please bring me the Foster file." When she placed the file on his desk, he said, "Thank you, that will be all for now. Please, close the door."

He looked at her departing back and shoved the folder into the desk drawer. He leaned back in the chair and put his feet on the desk. This was something he had always meant to try. It felt good. As long as he didn't lean too far back. Now why did I do that, he wondered.

Marlene intentionally closed the door to her employer's office. She reached in her purse, removed her cell phone, and dialed the private number of Francine Michaels, Attorney at Law.

"Hello, Marlene." Francine answered the phone quickly.

"He's here. I talked to the trooper, Scott, this morning early, before I left home. Ash went to the emergency room yesterday morning, and again last evening, to see a Miss Scarlet O'Hara. Sounds like an alias to me."

"Scarlet O'Hara? That's just crazy. See what else you can find out. I'll be in court most of the day. Call me later."

The day passed quickly. Ash called and talked to Scarlet several times. She asked, "Did you call to check on me?"

"That is a possibility," he told her. She laughed.

He left the office at five o'clock. Francine had called earlier on his private line while he was meeting with a client. She left a voicemail, "I'll stop by the deli. Come on over for dinner."

At the end of the day, he took a meal to Scarlet and explained to her that he had to 'put out a brush fire'.

Ash drove along the streets of Royal on his way to Francine's house. As an only child, she had inherited the home of her parents. She had moved back into her childhood home, situated in one of the upper class neighborhoods.

He had not seen her in several days—not since his chance meeting with Scarlet O'Hara. They had talked on the phone daily, but he had not actually faced her. There was no reason for this feeling of guilt, but it would not go away.

He drove into her driveway, cut the engine, and exited the Hummer. He walked quickly to the door and rang the bell. She opened the door and greeted him with a peck on the cheek. He felt a definite chill in the air. They went into the kitchen where she was re-heating the lasagna and preparing a salad.

"This is very thoughtful of you, but we could have gone out you know. I'm sure you're tired after a long day in the office," Ash said.

"No, it wasn't too bad today." He noticed an edge in her voice.

Ash removed two wine glasses from the cupboard, placed them on the table along with plates and silverware, and decanted a bottle of Royal Red. Francine placed the re-heated lasagna from the deli on the table along with two salads. They faced each other across the dining room table. Ash suddenly realized they were like a married couple sitting down to dinner after a hard day at the office.

The lighted candles on the table flickered. Ash made several attempts at conversation. His efforts were useless and he soon abandoned any hope of a friendly atmosphere at the dinner table.

Finally, the meal ended. Francine removed the plates and silverware and poured another glass of wine for herself and Ash.

She asked, "And, where is Miss Scarlet this evening?"

Ash was startled. He had not given her Scarlet's name and had not told her that she was in his home. He wondered if she knew, and if so, how did she know. It had to be Marlene. He thought he had kept this business from his employees. Secrets were very difficult to keep.

"We need to talk about that. A car hit her at the Green Leaf Mall—she's all alone in town. I have tried to befriend her. She's just a kid."

"Yes, I understand all of that, but where *is* she?"

"She is at my house, now."

"Well, then why didn't you just bring her with you?" Her voice dripped with sarcasm.

"Francine, don't do this. As I said, she's just a kid. She needed help. I plan to put her on the bus as soon as Dr. Fielding releases her."

"And, in the meantime?"

"She will stay in my guestroom tonight." Ash spoke more sternly than he intended as he finished the wine in his glass.

There was no more conversation as they cleared the table and loaded the dishwasher.

Francine's voice was icy as she spoke, "Don't put the wine glasses in the dishwasher. As you know they are antique—I hand wash them myself."

"Yes, I know."

The chill was still apparent as they went into the living room—a charming room that reflected Francine's love of beauty. She had placed many of her mother's antiques among her own furnishings. She placed comfortable chairs strategically near the bookcases. Classics and current novels sat side by side on the shelves. The books revealed Francine's eclectic taste in reading material.

They watched the news on television and did not speak for several minutes. Finally, Francine spoke, "Under the circumstances, I suppose you will not stay the night." It was not a question. The chill in her voice caused his spine to crawl.

"No, I had not thought to spend the night. Francine, please understand. Can't you?"

"I'm afraid not. I'll just say goodnight." She arose and walked to the foyer. She opened the door. Ash followed her.

"Goodnight," he said. She did not respond as he walked to the Hummer, got in, and started the motor.

The road home seemed long.

Chapter 9

He heard her laughter when he entered the foyer, tossed his keys on the table, and went to the den. Scarlet sat cross-legged on the leather sofa—wrapped in the shawl from the back of the sofa. She seemed also to be wearing one of his tee shirts beneath a sweater he had bought in Ireland. Ordinarily, the fact that she had gone into his closet and selected items of his clothing would annoy him. It's strange, but he didn't mind at all. God only knew where her clothes were. She only had her purse at the time of the accident.

It was still early and a rerun of a popular show from the past played as he seated himself in the leather-upholstered recliner adjacent to her. She was rubbing her bare feet.

He asked, "Feet cold? I'll get you a pair of socks."

He arose, went into his closet, where he selected a pair of white cashmere socks, and returned to the den. She was still intently watching the re-run of an old sitcom. Ash unrolled the socks, and placed them on her cold feet.

"Is that better?" He wanted her to turn off the TV and talk.

Finally the commercial came on and she turned to him and said, "Ash, hi! Did you have a nice dinner?" Before he had time to answer she continued, "I enjoyed the chops you brought me. Minnie's has good food. Thanks."

"You're quite welcome. We need to talk. The doctor wants

to see you again in a couple of days. I need to know where you're staying so that I can take you to see him."

"I told you I'm staying near the mall. I can get a cab and not cause you any more trouble." She unwound from the sweater and continued speaking, "I'll get dressed and you can call me a cab."

"No, I think you need to stay here tonight. I'll take you to the motel in the morning. Tomorrow is Saturday and I'm free. You can see the doctor on Monday and then be on your way. How does that sound?"

"I don't want to be a bother."

"I insist. You stay here tonight and tomorrow we'll think about other arrangements. After all, Miss Scarlet, tomorrow is another day!"

"Oh, fiddle dee dee. You win. Now where do I sleep?"

"Fiddle dee dee?" Ash asked. "You must have seen the movie!" he added.

"I've probably seen that movie a thousand times. I guess you already figured out my mother loved it as much as yours. Now, again, where do I sleep?"

"That's settled, then. I'll check the guest bed. I have a housekeeper that comes in so there should be bedding already on it. I'll check. Come along with me."

She picked up her shoes from the floor and followed Ash to the guest room.

"Did you have a nice evening with your friend?" she inquired.

"Yes." No need to bother with details, he thought. Just leave it at that.

"Hey, Ash, I was wondering, do you have a girlfriend?"

"At this point, I'm not sure."

"Yes, well—tomorrow is another day."

Chapter 10

*A*sh awoke early. The first thing he noticed was the pleasant aroma of freshly brewed coffee. He hurriedly put on a pair of crisply ironed jeans, a polo shirt—with the proper logo and walked down the hall to the kitchen. He was pleased to see Scarlet, wearing his tee shirt from the night before. Two bowls filled with cereal were ready for the milk that she held in her hand.

"Good morning, Ashley," she greeted him.

"Well, good morning, Miss Scarlet. You seem to be greatly improved."

"I'm good as new. Hope you don't mind—I took a shower. I found a shower cap to protect the bandage. The sweater was too warm this morning so I'm wearing your tee shirt from last night. It's a good cover-up, don't you think?" She gave him a beguiling smile as she twirled for his approval.

"Very fetching," he said. The short tee shirt revealed two great legs. Why did I not notice that before, he wondered? Um, um, cute little butt too, he said to himself.

"I looked for eggs 'n stuff. I couldn't find anything but cereal."

"Cereal's all I ever eat for breakfast except the times I visit Minnie's and that isn't very often. Sometimes on Saturday I go to Mother's and she has pancakes for me."

"This is Saturday. Don't let me keep you from visiting your

mother. I know that's very important. I'll just hang out here. I really don't want to interfere with your life—anymore than I already have."

"No problem. You and my mother would get along beautifully. She'll be thrilled to finally meet Scarlet O'Hara."

They finished eating breakfast, rinsed the dishes, and placed them in the dishwasher. Ashley called his mother. She was delighted that he was coming and bringing a friend.

Scarlet appeared in the den—dressed and ready for the visit to Annette Wilkes.

Ashley inquired, "Do you need anything, make-up or whatever women need. We could stop and do a little shopping if you do."

"I could use a bit of makeup. I only have lipstick in my purse."

"I've called Mother and told her we'll be there about one o'clock. We have time to shop. Is the drugstore OK or do you want to go to one of the department stores at the mall?"

"The drugstore's fine. I just need a couple of things."

As they left the garage in the Hummer, they met the Winslow sisters coming in, and stopped to speak.

"Good morning, ladies, and Miles. You're out early."

"Yes, we had to take Mr. Belvedere to the vet. Poor thing has a kidney infection. That's not unusual with cats, I'm told."

"I hope he'll be all right. Is everything else going to suit you?"

"Yes, we're fine. Who is your friend?"

He didn't wish to relate the famous name and try to explain at this time. "We'll come up to see you later," he responded.

"Good, we'll expect you for cocktails about six o'clock. Miles will prepare a light supper also. Is that all right?"

"Wonderful! We'll see you then. Have a nice day," Ash responded.

"She's got a bump on her head. See that bandage?" Bella said as they moved into their assigned parking space.

Ash drove out of the garage. Once they were on the street, he explained, "I didn't think I had time to tell Miss Angela your name and then go into the explanation that would require. We'll just go down for cocktails this afternoon. They are lovely ladies, very old fashioned and you'll get a kick out of them. Guess what they do for fun on Sunday?"

"Go to church?"

"No, they watch NASCAR!"

"No way! Those old ladies? I don't believe it. You said they are old fashioned."

"It's true! As strange as it seems, trust me, it's true."

They stopped at one of the chain drugstores for Scarlet to get the cosmetics she needed. Ash went in with her and offered to pay for her purchases, but she declined his offer.

Back in the car, she removed a mirror from the purse and applied makeup, as Ash continued on the way to the home of his mother.

"We need to change the bandage when we get back to my place. Don't let me forget." Ash had not thought to change it earlier.

"I checked it last night. It's OK."

As he approached the home where his mother still resided, he was aware of the large, white columned house sitting on a hill of lush, green grass. Her flower garden was inside the circle of the driveway. He suddenly remembered the kitchen garden at the back of the house. She had planned it, dug it up, and planted it herself years ago. Today he wondered why he had never offered his help.

Annette Wilkes was a powerful influence on her only sons' choices in life. She was never demanding or bossy, but always there if he needed her. They developed a good friendship and enjoyed the time they spent together. He didn't feel that it was an obligation to spend time with her on Saturday and very often drove out for a visit.

As he turned into the driveway, Ash noticed that Jason was

busy in the flowerbed. Jason looked up, waved to Ashley, and resumed his digging.

"That's Jason," Ash told Scarlet. He continued, "He knocked on Mother's door one day several years ago needing work. It was at the time that Mother's gardener had retired so she put him to work. He turned out to be a good worker and very knowledgeable. Several of Mother's friends hired him. He has a thriving lawn care business now. He's doing very well and was able to move out of his mother's house and get a place of his own. I see he has one of his helpers with him today."

Jason spoke to his helper, Chris, "That's Mr. Ashley, Mrs. Wilkes's son. He's a good guy. He helped me get started in business. He does my taxes and stuff."

"Who's that with him?" asked Chris.

"I don't know, but it sure ain't Francine. She won't ride in the Hummer." Jason replied. He leaned on the spade. "This may be an interesting visit," Jason said.

Ashley and Scarlet got out of the Hummer and made their way to the front entrance of a somewhat smaller version of Tara than the one in the movie. Annette opened the door before he rang the bell.

"Ashley, it's so good to see you and who is this?" Annette said, as she offered her hand to Scarlet.

"Mother, you won't believe it. This is the long awaited Miss Scarlet O'Hara."

This confused his mother and for a few seconds she was speechless. She soon recovered and stammered, "Oh, I—well, I don't know what to say."

"I'm sure you don't, Mother dear, but she is the real thing. There she was, at McDonalds, looking for a place to sit with a tray full of burger and little pink packets of sugar and other condiments. I came to her assistance."

Scarlet spoke, "He's right, I really am Scarlet O'Hara. My mother loved *Gone With The Wind* as much as you do. She would be so happy to know that I had met Ashley Wilkes."

Annette was obviously confused as she led the way into the foyer. "Please come in. I have lunch on the terrace. Ashley, bring...," she hesitated over the name, "Charlotte out to the terrace." Ash chose to ignore his mother's confusion.

They seated themselves at the white wrought iron table on the terrace. The chairs were tiny, too small for Ash's long legs, but he managed to fit himself in. Annette served what she referred to as pick up food—raw vegetables and dip, sandwiches, tiny homemade corn muffins, assorted cheeses, and homemade brownies.

Ash was obviously enjoying the little fun he had with his mother, although he was not certain that she remembered her lifelong interest in the Margaret Mitchell book or the grand movie. She had told him many times about attending the movie in 1939 when she was in the fourth grade. It was, according to his mother, the first four-hour movie ever produced. Ash had given her a copy on DVD.

"How are the roses doing?" Ash asked. He observed that Jason and Chris had moved to the rose garden.

"They're still nice, but beginning to fade. Jason works so hard to keep them blooming. We have some new ones this year. I love the names they are given. We have one called Summer Wine. My favorite is Our Lady of Guadalupe," his mother replied.

"Gua-da-lu-pay." She stressed each syllable.

Ash briefly told his mother about meeting Scarlet, but she seemed to be confused and did not respond. Instead, she continued talking about the roses and calling them by name, "Eden, Lady Bird, and Agatha Christie." She tired of the game and became quiet.

After lunch, Ash took Scarlet on a tour of the grounds. She was especially interested in Annette's potting shed where her latest project was underway. Small pots of rosemary, dill, oregano, mint, and bay awaited their new home in the herb garden.

"Are you a gardener?" Annette approached Scarlet and asked.

"No, I don't have a place for a garden. My mother always had roses. She loved roses."

"Yes, Jason is working in the roses today. Did you see him? He's out by the fence working with the climbers."

"I'll go speak to him," Scarlet said.

Scarlet walked toward Jason. When he saw her approaching, he stopped cutting the dried blossoms and turned toward her. "Hey, I'm Jason," he said.

"Good to meet you, Jason. I'm Scarlet. The roses are beautiful."

"Yes'm, they surely are. I try to keep some blooming all the time. Mrs. Wilkes enjoys them so much. She takes these dead blooms and makes potpourri. I had a time learning that word—potpourri. She's helping me with my vocabulary, too. We do crossword puzzles together. She's a good woman."

"I'm sure she is. It's nice to meet you, Jason." Scarlet rejoined Ash and his mother for a final walk around the lawn and to the Hummer parked in the driveway.

As they said goodbyes, Annette whispered to her son, "Who is this young woman? Should I know her?"

This remark concerned Ash, but he did not know how to respond so he said, "Her name is Scarlet, Mother." He kissed her on the cheek and said, "See you soon."

When they arrived back at Ash's condominium, they went from the garage to the first floor unit where the Winslow sisters lived.

Chapter 11

*B*ella sat in the foyer on the small French provincial chair. She waited for the doorbell chime that would announce the arrival of that nice young man from upstairs.

She wondered. His name is Ashley Wilkes. I think I knew someone by that name years ago. Maybe not—he could have been in one of my soaps. I love the soaps but sometimes the telly—can you believe that's what Miles calls it?—the telly. What was I saying? Oh, yes, sometimes the telly is blurry. Even after the operation on my eyes and the glasses, Sister got for me.

My head is all mixed up today. Bella shook her head as if to clear the muddle. She continued her inner conversation; I hope he won't bring that awful Francine. I don't like her at all—not a little bit. She isn't good enough for—oh, shoot. What's his name?

Why does Sister enjoy those awful races? Cars speeding around the track and crashing against the walls. Papa was a racecar driver at one time—or maybe it was Benny.

I can't seem to remember. I'll ask Sister. I hope they will let me have a glass of champagne. Sometimes they do and sometimes they make me drink that awful diet soda. It won't be forever. Just wait until I get out of here and have my own place. I'll show them.

She clutched the pocketbook to her chest and smiled. She continued her wondering, just wait until Benny gets here we'll show them.

Chapter 12

*A*ngela heard the doorbell chime, turned the volume down on the television set, and started toward the door. She realized that Bella had also heard the chime and was on her way to open the door. Bella clutched the ever-present pocketbook, as she reached the door first and opened it to admit Ashley and his lovely friend.

Angela was first to welcome them as Bella stood quietly by. "Good evening, it's so good of you to come. I trust your mother is well. Please come in."

Mr. Belvedere greeted the visitors with his full attention to the leg of Ash's pants. His sniffs did not detect the hint of another feline, so he turned his attention to Scarlet. He found nothing of interest in the newcomers and soon ambled off to his pillow on the floor near Bella's chair.

Ash gave each of the ladies a kiss on the cheek, extended his hand to Miles, and spoke, "Yes, Mother is doing fine. I would like for you to meet my friend, Miss Scarlet O'Hara." He waited for their reaction, but none came. He continued, "She was in an accident. She got a bump on the head. No cause for worry."

The ladies and Miles ushered them into the drawing room where they had been watching a video of the NASCAR race from the previous week. Miles turned the television set off, moved to the bar, and began mixing cocktails. Bella watched him, anxiously hoping that she would not get a diet soda.

Scarlet and Ash selected chairs and sat down. Miles served the drinks from a silver tray along with hors d'oeuvres while Angela started up a conversation with Scarlet.

"Are you new to our little town?"

"I'm actually just passing through. I was involved in an accident and will be here another day or two. Fortunately Ash came to my rescue."

"Do you know Francine?" asked Bella. She was pleased not to have a diet soda.

Scarlet, bewildered by this question, turned to Ash before answering, "No, I don't think so."

"Oh, Bella, hush," Angela chimed in.

"I don't like her. She's not nice to me," Bella retorted.

Angela attempted to change the subject. "You might like to have Ash give you a tour of the winery while you're here. We are quite proud of Royal wines."

"I hope she's nice to Ash. I think he should court you and forget about that mean old Francine." Bella continued her tirade against Francine.

"Bella, I'll have to send you to your room if you can't be nice. I'm warning you." Turning to Scarlet, she continued, "Please forgive my sister. She is not well today."

"I am too. I'm just as well as you are—and a whole lot prettier. I danced every dance while you had to sit them out. The boys always liked me best."

Miles interrupted, "Come with me, dear. We'll see what's on the television. I'm sure we can find one of our programs." He turned to the visitors and explained, "Excuse us, please. It's time for our programs."

Bella became docile and followed Miles from the room. She still clutched the pocketbook. He quietly took her to her bedroom and turned the television on to one of her programs. She would be happy for a while.

There was a slight wait until the conversation resumed. Ash looked at Mr. Belvedere, resting quietly on his pillow. He asked

Angela, "How is Mr. Belvedere?"

"Oh, he's fine. The vet prescribed medicine. He will be all right in a few days. He is like his owners, getting on up in years," Angela responded.

Mr. Belvedere heard his name called. He looked up, yawned, and returned to his nap.

"Were you really watching NASCAR?" Scarlet asked.

"Oh, yes. We discovered, some years back, that our Papa was one of the first racecar drivers. It was kept secret as long as Mother was alive, but since we have learned about it—" she looked at Miles who had returned to the room and resumed speaking, "we take delight in the life he lived. You see, in addition to driving race cars he was also a moonshiner or a bootlegger … whatever you want to call it."

"I don't understand." Scarlet was confused. She found it difficult to associate these two elderly, refined ladies with a bootlegger.

"Papa started out making moonshine liquor. It required fast cars and drivers to out run the revenue agents. That led into racing and eventually to NASCAR. After we learned what he really did, we always told, when asked, that he was in the beverage industry."

Angela allowed time for that to penetrate and continued. "The question was always, 'Soft drinks?'. We would answer, 'not exactly'.

"Moonshine was illegal liquor that was made in a still. The revenue agents were always after the moonshiners. They called it moonshine—I suppose because they made it after dark in the shine of the moon, when no one was about.

"They used fast cars to outrun the revenue agents. A very famous racecar driver handled the deliveries. You would recognize his name if I mentioned it. The cars were what they called 'souped up'. I understand that means very fast. That led the way for racing and eventually NASCAR.

"Mama kept it all from us, but when she passed we became

51

interested to find out why we lived here in Royal and Papa lived in the mountains of North Carolina."

"Wow, that's so interesting. Tell me some more." Scarlet was interested now.

"Papa took good care of us after Mama moved us to Royal. He came to visit, but more or less stayed out of sight. I'm sure there was speculation about our wealth and status in the community. Mama provided us with a life of refinement and Papa provided the funds. His visits were wonderful. He wore the nicest clothes and took us to splendid places. I'm sure, there was speculation and gossip about us, but we were happy.

"Mother concocted a story that Papa lived overseas, or as she put it 'on the continent' but was always vague about where it was. He dressed beautifully and put up a good appearance when he was here. He was several years older than Mother. He made wise investments that allowed us to live a life of luxury. We are very fortunate that our Papa provided so well for us. Well, so much for that. What about you, Scarlet O'Hara—tell us about yourself."

"There isn't much to tell. After your fascinating story, mine would be very dull. May I have another one of those cheese thingies?" Ash noticed how easily she avoided the request for information about herself.

Miles reappeared to freshen their drinks and to pass the tray again. He announced that Miss Bella was not feeling well and would remain in her room. Ash and Scarlet stayed on for a light supper.

Miles had prepared a meal and joined them at the table. He was a very pleasant man with impeccable manners.

He asked Ash, "How far did you travel to find this delightful young lady?"

Ash responded, "To the nearest McDonalds." They all laughed at his remark.

"I detect an accent, Mr. Miles. Are you British?" Scarlet inquired.

"Just Miles, Miss. And, yes, I am British, although I have been in this country most of my life. I came here as a young lad to live with a relative in Virginia. When my relative passed, I was at loose ends until the Winslow family hired me. After living all these years in my adopted South, I have actually worked hard at retaining my British accent." Miles smiled as he made this confession.

"This roast is delicious! Where did you learn to cook?" Scarlet asked.

"Thank you. I've learned by trial and error. Originally, I hired on as a chauffeur. Of course, I was in charge of maintaining the family's vehicles as well as helping out in the house. In recent years as the household help became harder to find, I took on these other duties. The ladies put up with me now."

"Miles, you are too modest. We couldn't get along without you," Angela said. "I'll have another serving of those delicious potatoes."

Ash and Scarlet enjoyed the evening with the Winslow ladies and Miles, but left soon after dinner. They took the elevator to the third floor and entered the foyer.

Scarlet looked around as if for the first time and commented to Ash, "You really have a beautiful place here."

"Thank you. It's my sanctuary." He felt so much tenderness for the young woman who had landed in his life. He reached out for her and held her close as he began to stroke her long blonde hair. Suddenly he was kissing her and she responded.

"I'm sorry," he said as he released her.

"Why?"

He kissed her again. She ran ahead of him toward the hall that led to his bedroom. He followed.

Chapter 13

*B*ella is unhappy. Sister sent me from the room. I will have to stay here until they come for me. They won't let me go back to the drawing room. I hope they don't forget me. Miles won't forget me. He always remembers. I'm hungry. It must be near time to eat. I suppose I did something naughty—I wish I knew what it was. I guess I will just go to bed and wait for Miles to come and get me.

She moves to the bed, still clutching the pocketbook. She turns its contents out on the coverlet, and very carefully looks at each item. There's that friendship ring—Benny Carlton gave me that ring. And, the dance card from the ball—I put it in the plastic bag. It looks like new. Oh, and the lace handkerchief Papa gave me to go with my pretty dress. A roll of mints—I don't remember them. I guess Benny gave them to me. And, here's my money. I forgot how to count. I don't know how much money I have but I hope it will be enough. For when Benny comes to get me.

"I'll show them. I'll show them all. They think they are so smart—I'll show them." She spoke aloud.

She carefully replaced the items in the old pocketbook, snapped it shut, turned back the coverlet, and crawled in to bed with her clothes on. She was soon fast asleep. She dreamed of Benny Carlton and was happy.

Chapter 14

When morning came and Ash awoke he was, at first, surprised to find Scarlet in his bed. This was unusual for him and he had to come to the realization that she was real. She turned toward him and moved her arm across his chest. He took her hand and kissed it softly until she awakened and smiled at him.

"Good Morning," she said.

"You're lovely—even as you wake up—all tousled and sleepy-eyed."

"Thank you. You are so sweet."

He slid out of bed and found a robe for himself and one for Scarlet.

He sat back on the edge of the bed and said, "I didn't mean for this to happen."

"I know. It's all right. Let's get the coffee going and have breakfast. Then we can talk about it."

He slid his feet into the leather slippers that were on the floor at bedside. She walked barefoot as they went down the hall and into the kitchen. He made coffee while she found cereal, bowls, and milk. She set two places at the table and they sat down to eat.

When they finished the meal, she cleared away the dishes, walked to the door, and said, "It looks nice on the balcony. We could take another coffee and go outside, if you want."

"Yes, that will be nice."

They poured two more cups of coffee, went out through the French doors, and sat on the balcony.

"It's a nice view from here. I can see a church steeple among the tree tops."

"Yes, that would be the Methodist Church. There has been some speculation as to who has the tallest steeple—First Methodist or First Baptist and I think the Methodists won. I suppose Mother is there, now. She usually goes to the early service. Sometimes I join her."

"Ash, I'm not sorry about last night. It was wonderful and I..."

He interrupted, "No, don't say anything more. I have no regrets and I hope that you don't either."

"No regrets. Now, it's a beautiful day, let's get out, and go somewhere. See the sights. Why don't you show me some of those vineyards?"

"Yes, that will be fun. I'm not sure if the picking is over for the season. Probably so, but we'll check it out. Would you like to get your things from the motel first so you can change clothes?"

"Ash, there is no motel. I haven't been truthful with you."

He ignored her statement that she had not been truthful. He said, "Do we need to shop for clothes? We can do that."

"I have a rented locker at the mall. I have a few things there. It doesn't hold much so I don't have much with me."

"I think it's time for you to come clean with me. I need some answers."

"Yes, I know. It's a beautiful day. Let's enjoy it. Tonight I'll tell you everything."

"Agreed. In the meantime—let's shower, dress, and go get your things. And, tonight, you can share your story with me."

He got up and went to her, lifted her out of the chair, and very tenderly kissed her.

When he released her he said, "I'll get the first aid kit and see if we can reduce the size of that bandage. OK?"

"No, I have a better idea. Let's get in the shower. I'll wash your back and you can wash mine. Then we'll change the bandage."

Chapter 15

Traffic was very light on this Sunday morning as they headed to the mall. The stores would not open until after church services. At one o'clock, the mall would be an entirely different place. Shoppers and onlookers would fill the stores. At this hour, there was no noise, no canned music, no exchange of money, and no flash of credit cards. She showed him where to park—near one of the entrances.

They got out of the Hummer and entered the nearly empty mall. She led him around the lower level to a place near the rest rooms to a row of lockers. She dialed the numbers into the lock and the locker opened. She began looking through the bags, apparently making decisions as to what to remove.

Ash said, "Bring it all. Don't leave anything here."

"Are you sure?"

"Absolutely."

There was a small suitcase and several shopping bags. Ash carried the bags to the Hummer and stowed them in the back. They left the mall.

He drove around the area and showed her some of the vineyards, although the picking had already begun. She delighted in anything new. He drove by his office. He pointed out to Scarlet that it had been his home when he was a child.

Soon he returned to the condominium. In the garage, he noticed that the car belonging to the Winslow sisters was not in its regular space and thought they must have gone for an afternoon drive. Sometimes when Bella was extremely agitated, a ride around town would soothe her. Ash remembered his mother telling him about the women as young girls. Angela was always the quiet one while Bella, who he believed was several years younger, was more adventuresome.

Chapter 16

*A*sh selected a bottle of wine from the wine cabinet, decanted it, and filled two glasses. He went into the den. Scarlet sat on the sofa ready to tell her story. He handed her a glass of wine and sat across from her in the leather recliner. There was a pause before she spoke—as she searched for the words that would explain her presence in this small town of Royal, North Carolina. Suddenly the little girl was gone. She began her story in very grown up terms.

"My mother and stepfather, Jim and Marjorie O'Hara live in Carrollton, Virginia, just over the mountain. I grew up there—finished high school, and took some courses in design at the community college. I got a job dressing windows at a mall in Richmond, met, and married a young man. The marriage didn't work out. We divorced and I stayed on in Richmond. There isn't much to say about the marriage. We realized our mistake early on and parted as friends.

"I've never known anything about my real father. Whoever he was, he gave me away. My mother refused to talk about him in any way. This led me to believe he must have been the world's greatest rat.

"Several years ago, while I was visiting Mother and Dad, I was rummaging in the attic and ran across a photo album that I had never seen before. Naturally, I opened it. I began thumbing through the pages. The pictures were beginning to fade. Some came unglued and fell out of the book when I picked it up. They must have been made during the late seventies or eighties because the clothing the women wore was dated and tacky."

She paused, sipped the wine, set the glass down, and resumed speaking. "I didn't think much about it at the time. I picked up the pictures that had fallen on the floor and replaced them in the album. I closed the photo album and went back downstairs. My visit ended in a few days and I returned to Richmond.

"Last month my mother passed away and I came home. I stayed on a few days after the funeral. Dad and I went through some stuff in the attic, to see if I wanted anything. We ran across the photo album. Dad opened it. He turned a few pages, handed it to me, and told me I should have it. He always treated me special. We have a good relationship. I've always called him Dad. I'm Scarlet O'Hara because he legally adopted me."

"What was your father's name? Who are you, really?"

"I don't know. Mother would never tell me and there was no record of him in any of her papers. I never worried about it before, but after Mother died, I really needed to know. I went to the courthouse and searched the records of births. There is no record of my birth in the county."

"You looked at all the births for that date?"

"Yes, but I don't know what name was used. I don't really know where I was born. Even the date could be wrong. I came to a dead end. That's when I became determined to know who my real dad was."

Ash looked thoughtful and said, "It seems to me you could have asked your stepfather, Jim O'Hara."

"That sounds reasonable." She paused and added, "I couldn't ask him, I was afraid it would hurt his feelings. He's been so good to me—I would have trouble asking him about it."

Ash walked to the window and gazed at the setting sun. The western sky seemed to be ablaze. He stood there a few moments trying to come up with something he could say that would be of help to her. Nothing came to his mind. He poured another glass of wine for himself and Scarlet and returned to the recliner. He waited for her to begin speaking again. She remained quiet.

He spoke, "What led you to Royal?"

"You won't believe it. It was Doc Hadley."

"Doc Hadley? You mean he's—"

"In the photo album, some of the pictures were labeled with names and dates. There were three pages of pictures with similar backgrounds made on the same day. The picture labeled Richard Hadley had fallen out the first time I found the album. I googled the name and came up with several. One was in Royal. So, I came here first. I flew from Richmond to Mom and Dad's so I didn't have my car. I came here on the train—Amtrak."

She sipped the wine and began again, "I made contact with him, but didn't mention the album, pictures and stuff. I wanted to feel him out before I brought up the pictures."

"How did you find him?"

"In the telephone directory—he's listed as R.A. Hadley. I found his house, saw that old red truck, and waited on the corner for him. I watched for the old red truck. When I saw it, I put out my thumb, smiled prettily when he passed by, and he pulled over. Piece'a cake!" She was pleased with her ingenuity. She continued, "I didn't bring up any of this mystery. Build a relationship, I think they call it, and then go for the kill.

"We had talked about Facebook and he mentioned that he had a computer, but had not learned how to use Facebook. I suggested that I could help him with that. After a little prodding from me, he agreed to meet me at the library so I could instruct him on Facebook. I never made it to the appointment because a car hit me. I need to get in touch with him and make another appointment."

"Scarlet, your resourcefulness amazes me. You don't think Doc Hadley is your father, do you?"

"No, no he's much too old, but his picture is in the album so he must have known Mother at some time. I thought, maybe his son?"

"He does have a son, but he lives away from here. I'm not sure where he is, but we could find out. I'm sure my secretary will know. Not much escapes her."

"So, that's my story. It's pretty simple."

"Yes, it is. So, why all the intrigue? Why couldn't you just tell me why you're here?"

"I don't know who I am. I need to find out. I'm a giveaway and I need to know who gave me away. My funds are low—I've been away from my job for over a month and I'm running out of money. I didn't want you to know where I'm staying."

"Can you tell me now?"

She looked at the floor for several seconds before replying, "Yes, you know the storage facility on the access road near the mall? It's called Extra Space."

"Yes, I do."

"They needed someone to watch it at night after eleven o'clock, so I'm staying there at night. It isn't dangerous or anything. They pay me a small amount. If I see or hear anything, I just need to call the police. It's temporary until they find someone and by then I'll be gone."

"Storage units! I hope you didn't prowl around the lot. Did you stay in the office?"

"Yes. I had to call after the accident so they could replace me. I have a few things still there that I need to get."

"Scarlet, you're very resourceful, but it seems to me you live rather dangerously."

"You don't know danger! I stayed in that fleabag motel out on the interstate the first night I was here. I didn't get a wink of sleep. There's more going on in that place than you can even imagine. Drug dealers, prostitutes—I don't know what all. I couldn't wait until morning so I could get out of there."

He looked skeptical so she added, "Trust me; I was safer in the storage place than I was at the motel."

"I'm pleased to have the whole story out in the open—that

you trusted me enough to confide in me. I'll do anything I can to help you. We'll get your things from storage after you see Dr. Fielding." Ash sat quietly for a few minutes before saying, "Scarlet, you've searched the records in Virginia, how about North Carolina?"

"No, I just assumed I was born in Virginia. Mother and Dad are both Virginians. They've never lived anywhere else so I thought—I see what you mean. I wonder if I can search birth records online."

He crossed the room, took her hand, and said, "Scarlet, let me help you. We can solve this puzzle together."

She arose from the sofa and they embraced. He held her for a moment and kissed her tenderly. He silently vowed to see her through this quest.

Chapter 17

On Monday morning, Ash went to his office leaving Scarlet sleeping soundly. The housekeeper would be coming today. He had some uneasiness about leaving Scarlet in his bed for her arrival. Scarlet slept soundly and looked lovely. He did not attempt to wake her.

Marlene was astounded when he arrived at the office in such a cheerful mood. She commented on his light step and the fact that she had never heard him whistle. He greeted everyone by name, entered his private office, and tossed his briefcase onto the leather sofa. He sipped his Starbucks coffee, bit into the chocolate filled doughnut, and buzzed Marlene to come into his office.

"Good morning, again, Marlene. Please get me all the information you can find on Doc Hadley. Excuse me, Richard Hadley. How long he's lived here. Who his offspring are, anything you can find about him. He's on Google.com, I know for a fact."

"Doc Hadley? Why do you need to know about Doc Hadley? I could probably fill you in on anything you don't already know."

"I'm sure you could, but, please google him. Chop, chop."

"Yes, of course." Marlene left his office in a state of bewilderment. He could hear her tapping the computer keys.

He called Scarlet at his house, after waiting long enough for the housekeeper to arrive, so that Scarlet would be awake. She answered on the first ring.

"Good morning. I didn't want to leave you this morning, but the wheels have to keep turning. I admit I'm not really interested in being here this morning. I may cut out at noon and we can go on a little afternoon trip. Would you like that?"

"Oh, yes! It sounds like fun. I need to get my clothes laundered first so I'll have something to wear. They've been in those bags for several days. Is jeans and a shirt OK? Your housekeeper offered to do them, but I'm doing them myself so she can do her regular cleaning. I'll be ready when you get here."

"Wear whatever you want. I'll be there a little after twelve." He replaced the telephone on its base and began to whistle again. He knew that would tear Marlene up!

At twelve noon, he announced to Marlene, "I'm leaving for the day and will not be available by telephone."

"What if there's an emergency?" Marlene made no effort to conceal the fact that she was extremely agitated over the actions of her employer.

"Emergency? What emergency? Just deal with it." Ash retorted.

He loosened his necktie and threw the jacket over his shoulder. This was something he had always wanted to do. He whistled as he left the office. As he reached the Hummer, he turned toward the window, and saw his staff lined up at the window, watching in amazement. He waved at the staff and enjoyed the scramble as they hurriedly moved away from the window. He had never done anything like this before. He felt good! He was even feeling a little reckless and drove faster than the speed limit all the way home.

He parked in front of the building, used his security card to enter, and took the stairs two at a time to the third floor. He entered the foyer of his condominium just as Scarlet was tucking her freshly ironed white shirt into the waistband of her jeans. He was so happy to see her!

Suddenly, the housekeeper appeared in the doorway exclaiming, "Mr. Ashley, I don't know where you found this young'un, but you better hang onto her. She's a real jewel! She's been working right alongside of me all morning. You jus' pay me half wages today!"

Ash laughed at the idea of paying her half wages as he went into his dressing room and put on freshly ironed jeans and shirt. He called to Scarlet, "Take a jacket."

"OK," she responded. She knew she didn't have one in the bags they had rescued from the locker.

In a short while, they were on the interstate heading west. In the distance, off to the side, they could see the vineyards. A little farther on, the apple trees were loaded with fruit, not yet ready for picking. When the time came many of the townspeople came to help in the harvest. It was a happy time for them. Ash thought he might join them this year. That would surprise the natives, he thought. To Scarlet, he said, "I was just thinking, I may join the pickers this year."

"Pickers? What do you mean?"

"Some of the townspeople show up and help harvest the apples and grapes. I've seen them in passing and they seem to have a good time. Yes, I believe I'll pick this year."

"Ash, may I say something and not offend you?"

"I'm not sure, but you can try!" He smiled as he spoke.

"That first day in the mall—I thought you were a real stuffed shirt, but you know what? You aren't so bad, after all!"

"I'll take that as a compliment." He reached for her hand and drew it to his lips. He continued to hold it as he zoomed along the interstate.

Chapter 18

Soon they were in the foothills and Ash realized they had not had lunch. He began looking for a restaurant. Since he had been in the restaurant business, he had become critical of other restaurants. He was very often displeased with the service. The billboards along the highway advertised one that particularly appealed to him. He began watching for it. It was at milepost 299, only two miles away. He turned to Scarlet and asked, "Are you hungry?"

"Starving," she replied.

"We'll stop soon. What sounds good to you?"

"I'm not hard to please. You choose and I'll be happy with whatever you decide."

"Promise?"

"Promise."

When they reached Milepost 299, he left the interstate, followed the signs, and turned into the nearly empty parking lot. He glanced at his watch and saw that it was mid afternoon. No wonder they were starving. He stopped the Hummer, and Scarlet jumped out on the passenger side, as he exited from the driver's side.

He hurried to the restaurant door and was able to hold it open for her.

"Thanks," she said, "I appreciate your good manners. Your dad taught you well."

The waitress arose from her vigil in the back booth and greeted them warmly, "Come in, folks. Welcome to The Crest."

There were still a few late diners and Nina, according to her nametag, led them to a table near the window. There was a good view of the mountains in the distance. They could see a small brook flowing just outside the window.

"Been traveling long?" Nina inquired.

"No, just a little afternoon drive."

She handed them menus and left to allow time for them to look over the offerings.

"What looks good?" Scarlet inquired.

"I'm thinking mountain trout."

"Yes, I'm thinking that, too."

Nina appeared with tall glasses of fresh mountain water and spoke, "Do you need more time?"

"No, I think we have made a quick decision. We will have two mountain trout dinners with cole slaw, baked potatoes, and sweet tea to drink."

"Coming right up." Nina retreated to the kitchen.

"I've been thinking of buying a mountain getaway nearby," Ash said.

"Sounds nice. Have you looked around for a spot?"

"I'm thinking near the lake."

"So you could fish?"

"Not really. I'm not much on killing animals. I just like to be near the water. It has a calming effect on me."

"You seem pretty calm to me. You don't get your feathers ruffled, even though I've given you enough reasons. It hasn't seemed to have affected you, as far as I can see."

"Most of the times I have difficulty showing my inner feelings, but you haven't really done anything to upset me. We've done well together, don't you think? We're off to a good start!"

"Yes, but I'm going to have to get on with my search and

get back to my job." She paused briefly and added, "I need to know who I am."

"I've asked my secretary to search online for anything pertaining to Doc Hadley. If it's there, she'll find it. Trust me on that."

"I told you I went to the library—the afternoon, after we met at McDonalds."

"Yes, I believe you mentioned it."

"I researched Richard Hadley online and found very little. I also went through the newspaper files and found the usual news items. There was no reason to get excited. His wedding, death of his wife and," she paused, "well, that was about it."

"Was there something else?"

"Was he the coroner at one time?"

"If he was coroner, I don't remember it. If so, I'm sure Marlene will find it."

Nina arrived with their lunches. She very carefully placed each dish on the table, stepped back as if to examine her handy work, and asked, "Anything else?"

"This is fine. Thank you," Ash responded.

He tasted the trout and found it delicious.

"Fresh from the brook, I expect," he announced.

"Excuse, me?" Scarlet looked puzzled.

"The trout—freshly caught I'm sure. I saw a stream back down the highway. This is a great place for trout fishing."

Scarlet nodded in agreement.

They finished the meal, returned to the highway, and headed up the mountain. They enjoyed several scenic overlooks and stopped at a gift shop. They bought funny hats with fishhooks hanging from the edges. Ash couldn't remember ever feeling so silly.

The air became chilly as the sun started to set and he bought Scarlet a hand knit wool sweater. He remembered reminding her to bring a jacket, not knowing that she didn't have one in the items rescued from the locker.

He noticed three log cabins behind the gift shop. It was such a romantic setting, with the lake behind the cabins, and the mountains toward the west. Ash, who had never done anything spontaneously, turned to Scarlet and asked, "Would you like to stay the night here in one of the cabins?"

"Yes, I'd like that." She put her arms around him and added, "You do come up with the best ideas!"

"Do you need to call someone?" Scarlet inquired.

"I have no one to answer to. Let's see if there's a vacancy."

Fortunately, there was a cabin available. Ash could hardly believe he had suggested this 'out of the blue' plan. He had never in all his life done anything so spontaneously. He always planned trips weeks in advance, but this came so easy to him. It did not bother him that they didn't have a change of clothes.

Mrs. Parks, the owner of the cabins and gift shop, asked that they give her a few minutes to check the cabin. It had been a busy day and she wanted to be certain that everything was ready. "I'll check on the firewood. You may need a fire tonight. The mountain air gets pretty chilly."

Scarlet raised an eyebrow and asked, "Did you plan this? You told me to bring a jacket."

"I'll never tell." He was beginning to develop a mischievous grin that Scarlet loved.

Ash parked the Hummer in front of the cabin. Mrs. Parks stepped onto the porch and called out, "Everything's fine. I lit the fire. It will soon be cozy. Have a good night." She walked back up the hill to the gift shop.

They got out of the Hummer. Ash took Scarlet in his arms and kissed her. "Miss Scarlet O'Hara, you have a powerful effect on me. I hardly recognize myself. I like me this way."

Chapter 19

*A*shley Wilkes puzzled Marlene. He had never taken off in the middle of the day before. You could just bet it had something to do with that girl—that Scarlet person. Marlene had always regarded him as the stuffiest person she had ever known. Now suddenly something had come over him. He was positively human.

Marlene had made it a point to telephone Scott Barnes, the state trooper. She was able to pick a small amount of information about her employer's activities on the recent morning when he was a visitor in the emergency room. Of course, Francine was the first to hear this tidbit of news. Marlene wondered what Ash is up to today and why this sudden interest in Doc Hadley? After she looked at her watch, she decided that Francine might be in court. She would wait and call her later. Better still, she would call tonight when she would have more information.

Now what in the world did Mr. Ashley Wilkes need to know about Doc Hadley? With him, you never know.

She made a fresh pot of coffee and poured a cup for herself. She sat down at the computer, logged on, clicked on Google. com, and typed in the name. She waited until the screen came up with a few references to Richard Hadley.

Some of the references included the word 'Doc'. There wasn't much of interest on the first page. Marlene already knew that he had served as coroner at one time. She scrolled down until something caught her eye. Richard (Doc) Hadley: He raced and collected vintage automobiles. "Who knew? That must have been a long time ago, before I came to Royal." Marlene spoke aloud.

Chapter 20

*D*inah removed her apron and cap, ran a comb through her hair, and clocked out. She was tired after a day's shift at Minnie's restaurant. She walked across the parking lot toward her old Dodge, hoping it would start without having to ask Minnie's husband for a jump-start. Her feet hurt. Of course, her feet nearly always hurt.

She had hoped that after the boys finished college she would have been able to quit work. With a little help from Tony and James, she could have lived on her social security check. That had not happened. Those ingrates seemed to forget about her and the hours she put in waiting tables to get them through college. Their father—she had divorced him—helped at times, but it was mostly Dinah.

She applied for all of the financial assistance available and provided the balance herself. Now she was getting too old to stand on her feet and wait tables. Nobody knew what agony she was in—her back and feet hurt and just about everything else.

The old Dodge started the first time. She moved onto the interstate for the drive to her home. Some home, she thought, I've lived in that room at the top of Miz' Olsen's house for ten years. I've shared the bathroom with another person, a man at that. I had to clean up the mess he made shaving. All those little hairs he left in the basin. The toilet seat was another matter all together.

Most days her lot in life hadn't bothered her, but today she was 'in a fix'. She was too tired to work and too needy to retire. Dinah felt like crying, but that wouldn't do any good.

"Buck up, old girl and smile. You can last a few more years," she said aloud.

She stopped at the convenience store for a pack of cigarettes. Lordy, she knew she ought to give them things up, but a girl had to have a little enjoyment. She's been smoking them all her life. She guessed if they were going to kill her, she'd already be dead and buried.

She pulled the little Dodge into her space in the backyard and climbed the outside stairs to her room. She wished she had a room on the ground floor. Miz' Olsen promised her the next one that came available.

She fumbled in her purse for the keys, unlocked the door, and swung it open before she saw the letter laying on the ratty carpet. She picked it up. It's from Tony. He's doing so well and she's very proud of Tony. She's proud of James, too, but things came harder for Tony. Maybe she petted him too much when he was a child. She did not prepare him for life.

She tossed her purse on the bed, sat down in the chair by the window, and read the letter. A check for one hundred dollars fell into her lap and she began to cry as she read the letter:

Dear Mama,

I've been thinking lately of how you have always looked out for me. I know you did without many things in your life so that James and I could have a better life. I want you to know that I appreciate all that you have done for me and now that I am working and making good money, I'm sending you a check for one hundred dollars. I plan to send you one hundred dollars every month. That with your retirement check should make things a little easier for you. If you need more, I can probably increase it. James is going to send you the same amount each month. I have a nice apartment near my job. I met a nice girl. Her name is Lindy. I hope to come home soon for a visit and bring Lindy with me.

Love, Tony

Dinah cried herself to sleep and awoke just in time to go to bed for the night. She had sweet dreams of James, Tony, and Lindy playing in a large backyard. They were all children.

Chapter 21

$\mathcal{A}$sh awoke before Scarlet and slipped out of bed. He reached for one of the provided terry cloth robes and tossed it around his shoulders against the chill. He checked the still burning fire in the fireplace, moved the logs around, and added another one to the blaze.

After making coffee, he went out on the back porch and watched the sun rise. The sun made a beautiful sight in the eastern sky as it was just appearing over the lake. The colors were vivid. He wondered why he didn't do this more often. His outdoor activities consisted of runs around his neighborhood, usually after dark, and an occasional tennis match.

There was a chill in the fresh morning air, as he sat in a rocker, put his feet up on the railing, and reminisced over the past few days. He reminded himself that Scarlet had not been back to see the doctor after her overnight stay in the hospital. They must remember to make an appointment.

He remembered what a good time they had the evening before. They had driven farther up the mountain to a restaurant and had dinner. It was a romantic place with a small combo playing soft music during the meal.

Scarlet expressed concern that they were not appropriately dressed, but he assured her they were fine. Imagine Ashley Wilkes saying jeans and shirts were fine for dining. His mother would not believe that he could do such a thing. He smiled at the thought.

He, suddenly, dozed off. The cup, held loosely between his thumb and forefinger, tumbled across the porch. Fortunately, the cup was empty and did not break.

Scarlet appeared, also wearing a terry cloth robe.

"Oh, did I startle you? I'm so sorry. Forgive me?" She kissed the top of his head. That had never happened to him before.

"Good morning, did you sleep well?" He stood up, retrieved the cup, and placed it on the small table near the chair. He wrapped her in his arms.

"Like a log," she said, "You?"

"Like a log. Are you hungry?"

"Just coffee will be OK. I suppose we need to start back. I'm sure you are missed," she said.

"I think I probably caused a sensation at my office. I'm always there. They must be in shock." He remembered how his staff had watched him from the window.

Chapter 22

Marlene parked in the parking lot behind the office, used her key to unlock the back door, and entered the building. It seemed unusually quiet as she removed her jacket, and prepared to make coffee. The telephone rang. She looked at her watch and realized that it was not time to open the office.

She spoke aloud, "Now, who can that be at this early hour."

"Wilkes Accounting," she said into the telephone.

"Good morning, Marlene. Just wanted to let you know I'm running late this morning. I should be in town in about an hour and another hour will get me to the office." He wished he could see her reaction to this bit of unusual news. There was no sound on the line. He could imagine her standing open mouthed, with the phone in her hand.

"Ash, is that you? Where are you?"

"Of course it's Ash. Who did you think?"

"But you're never late. Is everything all right?"

"Marvelous! Absolutely marvelous! See you soon!" He turned the cell phone off, clicked it shut, and placed it in its holder, smiling gleefully as he imagined Marlene's face.

"I think you just did something naughty." Scarlet smiled at him.

"Not I! Ashley Wilkes would never do anything naughty."

"I'm beginning to like you more all the time." She moved closer and squeezed his arm as the Hummer sped along the highway toward Royal.

Marlene immediately picked up the telephone, dialed Francine's cell phone, and left a message. "You won't believe it! I think they went on an overnight trip."

Chapter 23

At about this same time, Annette Wilkes woke up back in Royal. She rolled over and turned the alarm off before it had time to ring. She stretched her arms over her head, sighed, and got out of bed. Her slippers were on the floor. She put her cold feet inside the warm lining. It seemed that her feet were always cold these days. She put on her warm robe, padded downstairs to the front porch, and retrieved the daily newspaper. She read the headlines as she walked toward the kitchen.

She carefully cut out the crossword puzzle—laid the paper aside and set out two cups, two saucers, and two dessert plates. She decided to use her nice, linen napkins and carefully folded and placed them on the table next to the small plates. Jason would like that.

She sat at the kitchen table and began solving the crossword puzzle. She was good at the crossword. She usually completed the puzzle in five or ten minutes. In ink! She had Ashley doing them when he was nine years old. She wondered if he still took the time.

Did Ashley visit this weekend? She couldn't remember. Her memory was not as good as it once was. Was Ashley here or not? Oh, yes, he had a young lady with him. What was her name? She couldn't seem to remember that either. She'd have to ask the next time she saw him. It is very frustrating to realize that one's memory is failing. Oh, well, she wouldn't worry about that now. She'd worry about that tomorrow.

What was she going to do? Oh, yes, make the coffee. She went to the sink, rinsed out the glass pot, poured in six cups of water, measured three scoops of coffee into the filter, placed the filter in the pot, and returned to the crossword puzzle after turning the coffee maker on.

She began with the clue, one across, a satirical imitation. Oh, that's an easy one—parody. She filled in the blanks. One down, a human being. Another easy one—person. The coffee was ready. She laid the pen on the table, got up, and poured a cup. She drank it black with no sugar.

She heard a noise outside and realized that it was Jason come to work in the yard. There was always so much to do this time of year.

She went to the door off the screened in porch and called to him, "Good morning, Jason. Would you like a cup of freshly brewed coffee and a doughnut?" She knew he was particularly fond of doughnuts—the jelly filled ones. She tried to keep them on hand for him. He turned from the door to the shed and headed for the porch.

"Yes, ma'm, I sure would enjoy a cuppa." Jason replied as he very carefully wiped his shoes on the mat and entered the breakfast room. He loved this room. The breakfast room, separated from the kitchen by a counter, was bright and sunny. He and Miz' Wilkes had some good talks in this room sipping coffee and dunking doughnuts in her pretty dishes. His own mother did not have cups such as these. Bone china, he thought that was the name.

"Sit down, Jason. I'll be with you in a minute."

Annette poured his coffee and placed two doughnuts on the plate. "Here you are. How are you this morning?" She sat down and moved the puzzle aside.

"I'm good. How are you doing on the puzzle? Got 'em all?"

"Oh, no, I just started. I'll have to get you interested in the puzzles. You would be surprised at how it increases your vocabulary. I've done them all my life."

"I don't seem to have much time for anything like that. Thanks to you and Ash, I have about all the work I can handle. Even with my helper, we keep busy." He sipped his coffee before he dunked the doughnut. He continued speaking, "I saw Ash and a young lady here on Saturday morning."

"Were they here? I seem to remember Ash being here. I wasn't sure if there was anyone with him. Do you know who she is?"

"No m'am, but it sure weren't Miss Francine!"

"Wasn't Miss Francine."

"That's what I said." He didn't realize that she corrected his grammar.

She ignored his remark and asked, "Do you know who the young lady was?"

Jason was obviously puzzled. He had heard Ash introduce her as Scarlet somebody, but decided not to reply to Mrs. Wilkes's question. She seemed to be forgetful these days. Maybe he ought to call Ash and tell him about it. He sipped his coffee and ate the doughnut while Annette continued solving the crossword puzzle.

"You have to know a lot of words to do the puzzle," he stated.

"Yes, it builds ones vocabulary. Here's a good one, ten down, openly observable, six letters. Do you know what that is?"

"I'm not very good with words. I do figures better. What is it?"

"Overt. It also means easy to see." She filled in the squares. "Here's another one. A word you would use. Twelve across, a fabric for jeans, five letters, starts with a *d*."

She watched his lips move as he counted off five letters.

"Could that be denim?"

"That's right, Jason."

"Maybe I'll start doing those puzzles. I'm always looking for ways to improve myself. Now that I'm a businessman, I need a broader vocabulary. How's that sound?"

"It sounds good."

"I enjoyed the coffee and doughnuts. I need to get to work on those roses. They need spraying today. I saw some bugs on them."

"Aphids, Jason, aphids."

"That might be a clue in a crossword puzzle sometime," Jason said, as he left the kitchen and stepped onto the porch.

Annette made a mental note to buy crossword puzzle books for Jason. No, no, I need to write it down, she told herself as she picked up her shopping list from the counter top.

Annette finished her coffee, picked up the dishes, and washed them in the sink instead of starting up the dishwasher. It takes forever to get a full load with only one person.

Chapter 24

*A*nnette climbed the stairs to her bedroom. It had become her sanctuary since Cliff died. She redecorated the room in soft pastels—azure, coral, and ivory. The bookshelves surrounded the bay window. There was a comfortable chair in the window, faced toward the East. Many mornings she watched the sun rise. On sleepless nights, she sat and gazed at the stars, and dreamed of her beloved, Cliff. In the beginning, it was her reading nook. She doesn't read as much now that it strains her eyes.

She walked across the room, stepped on the plush ivory colored carpet, to the dressing room that Cliff designed for her. It held all of her clothing so that she did not have to go through the ritual of moving clothes as the seasons changed. Like most of her friends, she had far too many clothes. Also like most of her friends, she planned to give some of them up to charitable causes. She would take care of that soon.

She removed the robe and looked at her image in the large freestanding mirror. As usual, she was shocked at her aging body. God must have a sense of humor to have made us look like this in old age. Have I always looked like this? No, Cliff would never have loved this old shell. She began to cry.

Suddenly she put her nightgown on, said her prayers, slipped into bed, and wondered, why was it so bright outside. The moon must be full, she thought.

She began to think of a night long ago. She slept and her dreams were pleasant. She and Cliff were at a dance and Cliff danced every dance with her. She awoke and realized it was only a dream. In reality, Cliff would not dance. He thought he was too tall to be graceful on the dance floor. Even after taking lessons from The Arthur Murray Studio, he still would not dance. I won't dance, don't ask me ... that old song rang in her ears. No, Cliff would not dance with her that night, but she had a good time anyway.

It was the big New Years Eve Gala at the Royal Country Club. She and Cliff were to be married in June. She was young and beautiful. They had graduated from college and she wore the diamond engagement ring that Cliff had given her at Christmas. The wedding date was set for June 12. The band was playing all of those old romantic tunes. All of the fellows asked her to dance and, of course, Cliff did not mind. He wanted her to have a good time.

There was a young man up from Atlanta, visiting relatives. He was the quintessential young, tall, dark, and handsome. Annette hardly believed it when he asked her to dance. He held her close. She knew every step he made and followed him as though they had danced together forever.

The dance reminded her of the ballroom scene in one of her favorite movies, Madame Bovary. She compared their waltz to the one in the film of Gustave Flaubert's flaming novel of illicit romance and tragic ending. She and her best friend, Betsy Parker, had read the novel in secrecy because their mothers would not allow them to read such a trashy novel. Someone told her that she favored the young actress that played the part in the movie, Jennifer Jones.

What was the name of that young man? She thought at the time that she would never forget, but it seemed to have slipped her mind. She awoke with a start and wondered if it were time to get up. Looking at the clock beside her bed, she was surprised to see that it was nearly ten o'clock. She could not believe that she had slept so late. She pulled the curtains back from the window and saw that Jason was working in the roses. She must go down and speak to him.

Chapter 25

$\mathcal{A}$sh drove into the garage about ten thirty in the morning. He buzzed for the elevator. He and Scarlet ascended to the third floor. He quickly showered and changed into business clothes. Before leaving, he asked Scarlet to come into the kitchen where he had made coffee and filled two cups.

"I'm going to help you find your identity. I promise you that, but right now, I need to get to the office. I've been absent quite a few times just recently." He grinned at her. "Do you drive?"

"Yes, but I couldn't drive your car. I—"

"Nonsense," he interrupted. "I want you to make an appointment with Dr. Fielding and take my car if he can see you this morning. Call me after you make the appointment. Here's my office number." He handed her his card.

"Marlene will answer the phone and connect you to me. If it's at a time convenient for me, I'll come and take you to the doctor, otherwise use my car. Here are the keys." He put his fingers to her lips and said, "No buts. I assure you it's all right."

"I'll call Dr. Fielding's office and then call you."

"One more thing," he added, "sort your clothes and see if we need to go shopping. You may not have enough clothes with you for the next few days. I want you to stay, at least until we can find your father. OK?"

"OK. And, thanks."

He kissed her and was gone.

Scarlet sat down in the kitchen with the rest of the cup of coffee and tried to analyze what Ash said. He said, 'I want you to stay, at least until we find your father.' What did that mean? Would finding her father end this—this what? Life could be so complicated. She finished the coffee and picked up her purse to locate Dr. Fielding's card with his telephone number.

Or should I just disappear? she thought.

After talking to Dr. Fielding's office, she called Ash and told him the appointment was for four o'clock. He said he would be available to take her.

She straightened up the house, washed, and dried a load of hers and Ash's clothes. She showered and dressed in the freshly washed jeans she had worn in the mountains. She still had time on her hands. She decided to pay a visit to the Winslow sisters on the first floor.

Miles answered her knock and showed her into the drawing room. He spoke, "Good morning, Miss. I will tell Miss Angela and Miss Isabella that you are here. Could I offer you something to drink? I've just made a pot of tea."

"Yes, that sounds good. Just sugar, please. I'm waiting for Ash to return. I thought to ask about Miss Bella. She seemed so agitated when we were here on Saturday."

"Thank you, Miss. Miss Bella is fine today. She has good days and bad. I'll get your tea." He left the room.

Scarlet walked by the bookcases and read the titles, looked at the photos in small frames lined up in front of the books. One photo looked familiar. She picked it up for a closer look. The frame held three pictures. Surely, it was a coincidence. One of the pictures was the same one she had seen in her mother's album—Doc Hadley standing beside a car. The other pictures were of the same car and several other people, including Doc Hadley. Scarlet realized, as she looked at the pictures, that there was a definite link between Doc Hadley, the Winslow sisters, and her parents. She could feel the trembling in her hands.

As she replaced the picture on the shelf, Miles returned with the tea and placed it on a table beside a chair. Miles noticed when she quickly turned from the bookcase that the color had drained from her face. He wondered why the pictures had upset her. Is it possible…?

The sisters came quietly into the room and expressed their pleasure at seeing her again. "It's good to see you, Scarlet." Angela greeted her.

"Is Mr. Belvedere all right?" she asked. Her mind was blank. She couldn't think of anything else to say. She must not speak of the pictures. Wait until Ash gets home. He will know what to do.

Mr. Belvedere entered, as if on cue. He ignored everyone in the room and went to his pillow.

"Oh, he's fine. The antibiotics did the trick," Angela replied.

"We haven't seen you around the past few days," Bella commented. Bella seemed calm today. She still carried the pocketbook.

"We made a trip up the mountain, Ash and I."

"How nice. We have thought of going up a little later. We enjoy seeing the leaves after they turn to the glorious autumn colors. Perhaps in another month or two," Angela said.

"Have I come at a bad time?" Scarlet asked. "Maybe I should have called first?"

"No, no, it's quite all right. We're happy to see you. We were just getting ready for lunch. Will you join us?"

"I'm sorry. I'm just waiting until time for the doctor's appointment."

"Doctor's appointment? Are you ill?"

"No, it's a follow up after the accident. Just a bump on the head, but you know they always want to see you again. After the emergency room, I mean."

"Yes, we noticed the bandage on your head, but did not, of

course, call attention to it. Will you join us for lunch? Miles has prepared it and we would be so happy to have you join us."

"I'll just leave and come back another time. I should have called. No, no, don't bother. I'll just slip out."

She hurriedly made her exit and headed for the stairway, leaving the sisters obviously confused. She was out of breath when she reached Ash's home and had to sit for a minute in one of the chairs in the foyer. What she had seen was not possible. The photos in the frames were the same as those in her mother's album. What could this mean? She must find out more about Doc Hadley.

Chapter 26

Annette dressed and went downstairs to have breakfast. She was surprised to find coffee in the pot. Surely, she didn't leave it on all night. For some reason she was not hungry this morning, just a cup of coffee would be all she needed. Jason was at work. That's odd. He usually let her know when he started work.

Suddenly she remembered. She picked up the newspaper and saw that the crossword puzzle was nearly finished. The date on the paper was today's date. Could she possibly have already been downstairs this morning? It was all so confusing. She mustn't let anyone know. They would put her in one of those terrible homes.

What to do? The bed seemed the safest place for her this morning. She climbed the stairs, went back to bed, and cried herself to sleep.

Chapter 27

*A*ngela and Bella were alarmed when Scarlet rushed from the room. Miles seemed extremely distraught. Bella in her innocence asked, "What is wrong with everyone. Why did she rush out? That was very rude."

Miles led Bella back to the dining room. He seated her at the table, placed the napkin in her lap and said, "Here, my dear. Eat your salad. I must attend to something. I'll be right back."

He returned to the drawing room where Angela sat in one of the comfortable chairs. He approached her and said, "Miss Scarlet turned pale when she saw the pictures on the book shelves."

"Pictures? I don't understand. What pictures?"

"We have discussed removing them so many times. Who would ever believe that they would be recognized?"

"Miles please make sense. I don't know what you're talking about."

He walked to the shelf, picked up the frame with the three pictures, took it to Angela, and said, "She looked at these pictures, immediately became upset, and left."

Angela reached for her glasses on the table at her side, put them on, and looked at the pictures that Miles handed her. "Yes, these are the pictures we made of the Buick Park Avenue with Papa and Doc. And, the other young man—Benny Carlton. Why would that upset Scarlet?"

"I can only think of one reason. Don't you think she is about the age of…?"

Angela was obviously confused for a moment until she realized to what Miles referred.

"Stop, I can't hear this. That was all so long ago. Not now, Miles. Please not now." She began to weep. Miles realized that she had made the age association.

Chapter 28

*B*ella grew tired of waiting for Miles and Angela to come to the dining room for lunch. She ate a bit of her salad, decided to go to her room, and watch one of her soaps. They got mad at her for watching those trashy shows, but it was fun. There was so much kissing and hugging that always seemed to lead to something else that she could not understand. It involved lots of pawing, touching, and strange looking positions. Legs in the air and she didn't know what all.

Bella thought she could remember doing those things when she was young. Sister and Miles assured her she had never done anything like that. Still, I think I would like to, even now. She leaned back in the comfortable chair, and went to sleep. She dreamed of Benny Carlton. He is about the only one she has ever dreamed about before. It has become difficult to remember exactly what he looked like. He smoked cigarettes. She could still imagine the smell of the tobacco. It had lingered in her clothes so that she could smell him even after he went away. She liked smelling cigarette smoke. Sometimes Benny would let her smoke one, too. He smoked Chesterfields.

She remembered the last time she saw him. He was in Papa's study and Papa had come down from the mountain. They were both mad and Papa was trying to make Benny do something he did not want to do. Papa was trying to give him a car. Now isn't that strange. I wonder if Benny just got in that car and drove away. They thought I didn't know anything about it, but I knew everything. Mother didn't want me to see Benny and that is why she called Papa to come home. Sister, she was against Benny, too. They all were, even Miles. I've tried to get Miles to take me to Benny, but he won't. He has to do whatever Mother and Sister tell him to do.

I've been saving money for I don't know how long. When I can find someone to take me, I'm going to find Benny Carlton. Just you wait and see. I'll find him. I think I know just where he is. He's probably right over there in that park, waiting for me.

Chapter 29

Scarlet sat on the sofa in Ash's den and tried to envision the pictures she had seen in the small frames. One was identical to the picture she had seen in her mother's album. It was a copy of the picture with Doc Hadley. She believed the pictures were snapped more than thirty years ago, possibly in the late seventies or early eighties.

She went to Ash's computer and researched cars of that time. She logged on, clicked on Google.com, and typed in 1980's cars. After searching, she found it—a 1980 Buick Park Avenue. The car must be a piece of the puzzle that would unlock the mystery and lead her to her real father.

She heard the key in the lock, as Ashley opened the door, and stepped into the foyer. She ran from the den to meet him.

"Oh, Ash, it's all unraveling. I found the link. The sisters have the same picture that I found in my mother's photo album. It was the same car, a 1980 Buick Park Avenue and Doc Hadley standing beside it. He is the link. He has to be. What can I do, now?"

"Whoa, slow down. Say it again. What about the picture?"

"I went to visit Bella and Angela. The picture! It's the same. It's Doc. Oh, Ash. At last I'm going to find out who I am."

"Sit down and be calm. Start from the beginning."

She pulled him into the den and told him about seeing the

pictures. He sat still for a few minutes before answering, "This is very delicate. It's possible that Miss Angela and Miss Bella—I don't know. It seems too easy that you meet me and find your identity in this particular building. It's too coincidental. Did you mention it to anyone?"

"No, of course not. I fled the place. I'm sure they think something is wrong. I simply fled."

"Let's take this easy. It's time for your doctor's appointment. I think we need to keep it first, and then get your things from storage. After that—I think we need to talk to the Winslow sisters." He sat quietly and then added, "And, Doc Hadley, as well."

"If you think that's best. I can hardly wait. You can't imagine how anxious I am."

Chapter 30

sh drove into the parking lot of the medical building, parked, and went inside with Scarlet. She managed to stay calm as Dr. Fielding examined the wound on her forehead. He declared that the wound was healing nicely and also checked her vital signs. He applied a small bandage to her forehead. He did not feel that another appointment would be necessary, but encouraged her to call for one if she felt any ill effects from the accident.

They left his office and headed to Extra Space. Ash parked in front of the office and asked, "Do you want me to go inside with you? I'll wait in the car if you prefer."

"No, you can go with me. It's OK."

They entered the second floor office, where, according to the sign on the desk, Ruby Richards was the person on duty. She said, "Hey, Scarlet. We were so worried about you. What happened? We only heard that you were involved in a car wreck and were taken to the hospital by ambulance."

"Actually, I was not in a wreck, I was hit by a car. The driver was drunk. I guess I'll have to stay around and go to court."

"Oh, yes, you will. I heard it was Joey Baldwin. He's been in lots of trouble—drugs, alcohol, you name it and Joey has done it. I went to school with him. He's a good kid when he isn't drinking or drugging. You've come to get your luggage?" She got up, went to a closet, and pulled out a wheeled suitcase.

"We kept it safe for you," Ruby said.

"Thanks. I appreciate it. Have you found someone to work full time?"

"Yes, we have hired a young man. He's taking some classes at the college and will stay here from midnight until eight am, when we open. We appreciate you helping us out. Will you be staying in Royal?"

"I—well, I don't know yet."

"Stay in touch with us. Sara will be sorry she missed seeing you. Oh, yes, here's your check." Ruby reached into her desk, drew out the check, and handed it to Scarlet. They hugged and Ruby returned to her desk.

"Oh, this is my friend, Ashley Wilkes. Ash, this is Ruby."

"Pleased to meet you, Ash. I've seen you around."

"Nice meeting you, too, Ruby."

As soon as they were back in the Hummer, Ash said, "I need to check by the restaurant if you don't mind. Then we'll pay a visit to the Winslow sisters."

The restaurant had not opened for dinner. Ash used his key to unlock the door. Once inside he asked Scarlet to have a seat by the fireplace, while he attended to business. He was gone for a short while.

When he returned, he sat opposite her and began speaking, "My cashier has submitted her resignation. I thought if you were going to stay around, I could offer you part time, or temporary employment. It would be a great help to me, also."

"Ash, I can't make any decisions right now. I need to get this business finished. Even if I stay here, I'll have to go back to Richmond and take care of moving. I'm here because of my mother's death. I have my own business, you know. My assistant is dressing the windows while I'm away. I have an apartment, several loose ends to tie up."

"Of course, I wasn't thinking. You have a life."

"I thought I did, until now."

Chapter 31

When Ash and Scarlet were settled in the Hummer and out on the highway he said, "I need to make a quick stop at Mother's. Jason called. He is concerned about her mental condition. She seemed to be confused—didn't remember that we had visited on Saturday. He said she showed confusion on Monday when he came to finish in the yard. Lorraine, my sister, is out of town. She and the kids are visiting the in-laws."

He checked the time on his Rolex and continued, "It's dinnertime, now. We can check on Mother and then go back to my house. I know you're anxious, but I think we need to give Miles and the sisters time to have dinner before we pay them a visit. I have a hunch. I think we also need to talk to Doc Hadley."

"Yes, you're probably right. Apparently, he knew Angela and Bella's father, the bootlegger—and my parents, as well."

When they approached the driveway at his mother's home, Ash spied her walking toward the potting shed carrying a bag of organic soil. He drove around to the back of the house, jumped out of the Hummer and walked briskly to her. She was wearing a straw hat and an old shirt that had belonged to him, to protect her arms from the sunshine. She smiled and greeted him warmly. He was startled to find her apparently in a good frame of mind.

Scarlet was close behind him and called out to Annette, "Let us help with that large bag of soil. It's too heavy for you."

"Nonsense, I do this all the time. It's one of my loves—putting things in the ground and watching them blossom. The bag isn't heavy."

Ash took the bag and finished filling the pots while he talked.

"Are you OK, Mother? I've been out of town a day or two. Just came to check on you."

"Of course, I'm fine. You don't need to worry about me." She began placing geraniums in the pots. "Lorraine and Philip were here this morning."

"Are you certain they were here today?"

"Oh, yes."

"Mother, Lorraine, and her children are visiting her in-laws."

"No, I don't think so. That's next week. They visited me this morning. I'm sure of it."

"We've come to take you out for awhile. Let's go inside and take off that old shirt, and put on something else. Just leave the pots. We'll take care of them later."

"I have a dress on under this shirt. Where do you want to take me?"

Ash helped with the buttons on the shirt, removed it and the straw hat. He recognized the dress. It had been one of her designer dresses, and had plainly seen better days. Missing buttons and a frayed collar demonstrated his mother's disregard for her personal appearance.

He removed the gloves. Her hands were pitifully wrinkled and neglected. The nails were broken and dirty. He remembered what lovely hands she had always had and how the appointment with the manicurist had always been so important to her. He was saddened at the sight.

"Let's get a bite to eat and go to my house. Here, I'll put the shirt inside and lock the door. We won't be gone long." They guided her to the Hummer and Ash helped her into the front seat. Scarlet climbed into the rear seat.

Annette muttered, "I don't know why anyone would buy one of these big old vans. I can't even get in it without assistance. I need a comb and a tube of lipstick. A pretty rose color that suits my complexion."

Ash looked at Scarlet in the rearview mirror. She pulled the comb and lipstick from her purse and handed them to Annette.

"Thank you," Annette said. She combed through her hair and applied lipstick as Ash was leaving the driveway. She handed the lipstick and comb back to Scarlet, turned to Ash and asked, "Who is she?" pointing to Scarlet.

Ash replied, "A friend of mine." He drove to a small restaurant, where they ordered sandwiches and beverages.

Chapter 32

sh drove into the garage, parked the Hummer, and assisted his mother as she stepped from the vehicle. Scarlet hopped out of the rear seat unassisted. The three stepped into the elevator. Ash looked at his watch and thought the Winslow sisters and Miles would have finished dinner. They stopped on the first floor and rang the bell.

Miles opened the door and greeted them, "Good evening, please come in." He ushered the three into the drawing room and motioned to chairs. "Please be seated. I will fetch the ladies."

Scarlet sat on a small sofa. Ash and his mother chose the larger one opposite her. Angela and Bella entered the drawing room, accompanied by Miles. Angela was ashen and Bella looked puzzled.

Bella commented, "Is someone dead? Everyone looks sad."

"No, dear, no one is dead." Angela turned toward Scarlet and spoke, "I believe you were upset when you were here earlier? Would you like to talk?"

"Yes, or rather I would like to..." She found it very difficult to put her thoughts into words. "The pictures, over there," she pointed to the bookcase. "My mother has those same pictures—the ones in the small frames. I'd like to hear about them."

Angela arose and went to the bookcase. She picked up the frame with three photos in it, handed it to Scarlet, and asked,

"What would you like to know?"

"I believe that this one," she pointed to Doc Hadley's image and continued, "is Doc Hadley and he is also in the photos that my mother has. I believe—I don't know what I believe. Can you help me?" She handed the picture back to Angela.

"I'm not sure what I can tell you about the picture. The tall man, there by the car, is my father, Arch Winslow. He is the only one in the picture that I could identify. Other than Mr. Hadley, of course. I have kept the pictures because they are the only ones I have of my father. He was somewhat, shall we say, camera-shy because of his profession."

Scarlet was obviously disappointed. "I had hoped that you could identify the others in the picture. What can you tell me about it—anything at all?" she asked.

"No, dear, I've told you, it's the only picture I have of my father. That's why I so prominently displayed the picture. I'm sorry, I can't help you."

Suddenly, Bella arose, crossed the room to her sister, and took the picture into her hand. She looked at it for several seconds, adjusted her glasses, and said, "That's Papa." She pointed to him.

"Yes, dear that is our Papa." Angela's voice sounded strained.

Bella continued looking at the picture and made another announcement. "That one," she said, as she pointed to one of the younger men in the picture, "that one is Benny Carlton."

Miles very quickly and very quietly arose. He took Bella by the hand and said, "Now, now, dear. Don't worry about the picture. Come with me. We'll see what's on the television." He led Bella from the room.

Angela turned to Annette and remarked, "Mrs. Wilkes, we haven't seen you for awhile. It's good to see you again."

"Yes, it's good to see you," Annette replied. She didn't seem to know where she was.

"We've always admired your beautiful lawn and especially

the herb bed. Our mother had an herb bed. One of our maids made poultices and herbal remedies from the plants. Some of them were quite effective."

"Yes, I enjoy my herbs. Jason is helping me. We do crossword puzzles, too."

"How nice," replied Angela.

Ash stood up. "We must be going. We can show ourselves out, Miss Angela. I hope we haven't disturbed Miss Bella."

"She will be fine. Her attention span is very short. She has probably already forgotten the entire incident of Papa's photograph. Miles is so good with her." Angela arose as she spoke.

Chapter 33

*A*nnette, Ash, and Scarlet entered the elevator, pressed the button, and stood quietly as it rose to the third floor. They walked into the foyer and made their way to the den in silence.

Ash was first to speak, "Scarlet, how may I help?" Ash held her close. He smoothed her hair back away from the small bandage that she still wore.

"I don't know. I'm so confused right now. I suppose I need to sleep on it and try to sort things out in the morning. The car in the pictures at Miss Angela's is the same one in the pictures in my mother's photo album. The location seems to be different," Scarlet said.

She looked at Ash and inquired, "Will your mother stay the night? She could sleep in the guest room and I'll sleep on the sofa bed. She might be upset if I sleep in your bed."

"I doubt very much that she will consent to stay here. She's very independent. I'll see what she wants to do. I suppose she will be all right at her house. She's been staying there alone all these years since Dad died. Lorraine and I will have to come to some arrangement for her. Jason says he's worried about her. He's noticed that she's often confused. Doesn't remember our visit on Saturday. I'll go talk to her. I believe she is in the kitchen."

He kissed Scarlet softly and went into the kitchen. He found his mother removing clean dishes from the cabinet, rinsing them, and placing them in the dishwasher. He gently moved her away from the sink and said, "Mother, I would like for you to stay here tonight. You could sleep in the guest room."

"Where would the girl sleep? What's her name?"

"She is Scarlet and she will sleep on the sofa bed."

"I need to go home, Ash. You know I always sleep better in my own bed. Will you take me home?"

"Of course, if that's what you want, but we would be happy to have you stay here."

"Some other time, dear."

Ash, the good son, took his mother home, as she wished.

He knew it was a matter of time until she would have to move into one of the places she feared. Suddenly he had a gem of an idea. He would mention it to Scarlet.

Chapter 34

$\mathcal{N}$either Ash nor Scarlet slept well that night. Scarlet tossed and turned all night. It was toward morning when Ash finally slept. When he awoke at six o'clock, she was not in bed. He found her standing on the balcony holding a cup of coffee. She was gazing toward the sunrise.

"Good morning," he said and kissed her softly.

"I know I kept you awake and you must go to work." She rested her head on his shoulder as he stroked her tousled hair.

"Yes, I need to check in at the office for awhile. Because we didn't learn anything from the Winslow sisters, I think we need to have a talk with Doc Hadley. Can you call and see if we could see him about eleven o'clock this morning? I can be available by then. I just need to tie up a couple of loose ends at the office. Marlene can handle things for me. She is quite capable in spite of her, how shall I say it?"

"Nosiness? Is that a word?"

"I have to say she means well. I need to have a talk with her. Maybe later." He kissed the top of her head and went back into the condominium. Soon Scarlet heard the shower running.

She sipped her coffee and sat in one of the loungers. Suddenly she remembered something that Bella had said. It had slipped her mind until now. She had pointed at of one the men in the photos and called him Papa. She had pointed at a second person and called a name. Scarlet could not remember the name Bella had spoken. She would have to check that out.

She went into the kitchen and set out the cereal, milk, and bowls for a quick breakfast. When Ash appeared, he was not wearing his usual business attire. He had on khaki slacks, a polo shirt and tasseled loafers. Scarlet resisted the urge to comment on this new look. She decided to leave that for Marlene.

After breakfast, she followed Ash to the door. "What do you think of my new look?" Ash asked.

"I think you are very handsome and up to date. I can't wait to hear what your secretary has to say. I'm sure it will be original."

"You can bet on it. Be sure to get in touch with Doc Hadley." He gave her a quick kiss and went down the hall toward the elevator.

Scarlet cleared the table and put the dishes into the dishwasher. After she showered and dressed, she decided it was time to call Doc Hadley for an appointment. She went to the telephone and paused, should I mention Ash, or not—maybe not, she wondered. She dialed Doc's number from memory and waited for him to answer.

"Good morning, Doc speaking."

"Good morning, this is Scarlet. Do you remember me?"

"Yes, I do. I heard about your accident. Are you all right?"

"Well, news travels fast in this town! Yes, I'm fine."

"Yes, we have quite a network. Not much gets by us. Now, what can I do for you?"

"I'm available to help you with the computer. Sorry I wasn't available before. I could meet you this morning at the library. I'll probably be leaving in a day or so and I'd really like to help you get started. It won't take long. I could meet you today at the library about eleven o'clock."

"You're leaving, you say? In that case, I suppose I had better get a move on. I can change my plans and see you at eleven o'clock. I appreciate it, Scarlet."

"Great. I'll see you then."

Scarlet telephoned Ash on his cell phone.

"Good morning," he said.

"Hi, I just talked to Doc Hadley. I'm to meet him at eleven o'clock at the library."

Ash responded quickly, "Good, I'll pick you up at half past ten."

"I'll be ready. And, Ash, I just noticed all the clutter in this bedroom."

"Clutter? What clutter?" She could almost see him smiling as he spoke.

"It's mine. I'll get it cleaned up. My mother always told me I was a stranger to a clothes hanger."

"You know, she may have hit on something there."

Chapter 35

Scarlet walked down the stairway to the front entrance as Ash drove up at exactly half past ten. He started out of the car, but she waved him back, and opened the door herself. He frowned. She settled into the seat beside him and commented, "Doc will be at the library at eleven o'clock. I didn't tell him that you would be with me."

"Do you think I should give you a little time with him and then show up?"

"That might be a good idea. I can give him a few pointers on the internet. He wants some instruction on using Facebook. He's pretty sharp so it won't take long to get him started on it."

Soon they were at the library. Scarlet went in alone, while Ash went to The Soda Shop around the corner for a Diet Coke.

"Hey, Doc! Good to see you."

"I see you've still got a little bruise on your forehead. Did they get the driver?" Doc said, referring to the accident.

"Yes, I guess I'll have to stay around for his court date or come back later."

"I heard you were staying with that Wilkes boy. Annette's boy."

"Yes, I am. He is so nice—I have grown quite fond of him." Scarlet headed toward the computers. "Let's find a computer not in use and get you started."

Doc was a quick learner. She had him using Facebook by the time Ash arrived. Ash and Doc shook hands. Ash asked, "Doc, could we have a few minutes of your time?"

"Yeah, I guess so. Time's about all I have these days."

Ash led them to a small conference room. They entered and Ash closed the door.

"What can I do for you?" asked Doc.

Ash nodded to Scarlet and she began, "Doc, I'm searching for someone, and I think you may be able to help me."

"Who are you searching for?"

"I'm trying to find my father."

"What's his name?"

"I don't know."

"Sounds to me like you've got your work cut out for you."

"Yes, it looks that way."

"What makes you think I can help you?"

"Do you know Jim O'Hara?"

"Seems like the name sounds familiar."

"He's my stepfather. In other words he's married to my mother."

"Yes, Scarlet, I know what a stepfather is, but I'm sorry, I can't help you. Maybe you should talk to your stepfather. I've gotta go now. I thank you for helping me with Facebook. See you, Ash."

Scarlet was stunned into silence. She couldn't believe that Doc had left so abruptly. He definitely didn't want to talk about Jim O'Hara.

She turned to Ash. "What was that?" she asked.

"A man who had nothing to say about Jim O'Hara. Come along, we can't do anything else here." He led her out of the library and into the Hummer. He did not immediately start the engine.

"What do we do, now?" she asked.

Ash observed tears welling up in her beautiful blue eyes. He reached for her hand, lifted it to his lips, and said, "Doc knows more than he is willing to admit. He may have had a part in this mystery."

He started the Hummer, backed out of the parking space, and headed to a small restaurant nearby.

"What is a coroner?" Scarlet asked. "Is that the same as a medical examiner?"

"A medical examiner is a licensed physician with degrees in pathology and forensic pathology. A coroner is an elected official. It isn't necessary for him to be a doctor. Very similar to a medical examiner, the coroners do autopsies to support investigations of deaths. Doc Hadley was a coroner. I suppose the nickname of Doc is more or less an honorary title."

"Ash, is it possible that Doc had a part in my birth—or knows something about it? Are we getting close to an answer?"

"I don't know, Scarlet. Let's get some lunch and decide what we need to do next. We may need to talk to your stepfather. I know you don't want to hurt his feelings, but I think he could give us more clues to solve this enigma. Think about it."

"He'll be truthful with us. I'm sure of that."

Ash had reached a small restaurant near his office. He pulled into the parking lot and they entered the restaurant. Scarlet noticed two well-dressed women at the cash register in the process of paying their bills. One of them turned away from the register, busily replaced her credit card in her wallet, and froze in her tracks when she came eye to eye with Ash.

"Good afternoon, Marlene." Ash spoke.

As the other woman turned to face him, he spoke again, "Nice to see you, Francine." Neither of them returned his greeting as he turned to Scarlet, and with a mischievous grin, said, "I'd like for you to meet Scarlet O'Hara. Scarlet, this is my secretary, Marlene Carlyle, and my friend, Francine Michaels."

Scarlet stammered a greeting as Ash led her to a table near the window. Francine murmured something indistinguishable.

Marlene remained mute. They made a hasty exit from the restaurant. Ash enjoyed every minute.

Ash sat down, picked up a menu, and asked, "What looks good? I'm hungry."

"Ash, who is Francine? She's very attractive, for a woman of her age." Scarlet didn't realize what a barb she had just issued.

Ash laughed aloud. He said, "Scarlet, you are priceless."

"Marlene isn't bad looking—not at all what I had pictured." Scarlet picked up the menu. "What looks good?" she asked. "I'm starved."

Ash hid his concern over seeing these two together—it was a big surprise to him. Now, there is no doubt, where Francine gets information concerning his personal life.

"I'll have to teach Marlene a lesson," he muttered.

"What lesson would that be?"

"Stay out of the bosses' business. Now, let's order. I'm hungry, too."

Chapter 36

Following lunch, Ash took Scarlet back to the condominium. He parked in the front parking lot and went to the third floor with her.

"Scarlet, I think we need to pay a visit to your stepfather. Surely, he has the answers you need. Doc Hadley also knows something or he would not have left the library so abruptly this morning. Because he won't or can't tell you anything, the next step seems to be your stepfather. Do you agree?"

"You are probably right. I just don't want to ask him. Is there any other way to solve it? I don't understand all the secrecy. Adoptions happen every day. Do you understand?" Scarlet asked.

"No, dear, I don't. I promise I'll stay with this until we solve it. At this time, the best option we have is to see your stepfather. Did you ever talk to him about your adoption?" Ash asked.

She shook her head 'no' and said, "I always intended to ask Mother, but I waited too late. After she died, I thought I could find out on my own."

Ash continued speaking, "I'm available this weekend. I can go with you then. Think about it and let me know what I can do to help." He took her into his arms, kissed her, and reluctantly left the condominium.

Scarlet did not believe she could wait for the weekend.

Chapter 37

On the way to his office, Ash tried to think how he would handle the situation with Marlene. She was guilty 'by association'. When he saw Marlene and Francine together in the restaurant, he realized that she was Francine's source of information concerning his personal life. He wondered how long that had been going on. He couldn't think of any other tidbits she could have passed along through the years. Who knows what she and Francine had found interesting. He had never thought his life was interesting enough for this kind of intrigue.

He wondered how it happened that the two of them made this arrangement. They were not in the same social set. In fact, Francine was—he hated to think it—some sort of snob. He began to wonder what he had seen in Francine. As for Marlene, he decided that today he would act as if nothing had happened. Actually, nothing had happened.

When he arrived at his office, he parked in the back of the building, as usual. He went in the back door, stopped in the kitchen, poured a cup of coffee, and went into his office. There was no noise in the building. Even the canned music was quiet.

He went to the back offices. The staff had returned from lunch. Hal was playing with his cell phone and hastily stowed it in his pocket.

"Have you seen Marlene?" Ash asked. "Never mind, she's just driving up," he added.

Ash watched as she drove into the parking lot, parked in her usual space, and entered through the back door. Ash returned to his office, followed by Marlene.

"Ash, I owe you an explanation. Do you have time?"

"Marlene, yes, come in. We need to talk." He remained standing, as she sat primly on a chair facing Ash.

"I am extremely disappointed in you. It appears that you have compromised my trust. Your position in this office requires the highest amount of discretion—in personal matters as well as professionally. Our clients have the right to assume that we are trustworthy and discreet—as do I. In this incident with Miss Michaels—I trust that you have not betrayed my faith in you. I insist that you hold to our professional standards."

"Yes, Ash. Let me explain..."

"No explanation is necessary. Just one more thing—stay out of my personal business."

Without a word, she went to her desk, sat down, and resumed her usual duties, thinking to herself, this is not the end of it.

Chapter 38

fter Ash left for the office the following morning, Scarlet busied herself straightening up his bedroom. He was so neat and tidy that he must be unhappy to see her clothes lying about. So far, she had been able to contain everything in only one room. She found extra hangers and put her clothes in his walk-in closet.

She tackled the bathroom next. She organized her bottles, jars, and other containers of cosmetics into one of the empty drawers in the built in cupboard.

When her task was complete, she poured a cup of coffee and carried it to the balcony. She sat and reviewed her visit with the Winslow sisters. Miss Angela had explained the photograph, but there was no explanation of why Arch Winslow was in the photograph with Doc Hadley and the Buick Park Avenue car.

Suddenly she remembered Bella pointing at the photo and speaking a name. What was it? She tried to remember. Think about it, Scarlet. Run through a list of names. Think, girl, think. Do I dare go upstairs and ask? Probably not a good idea.

She remembered an old memory trick Dad used. When he mentally searched for a name, he would think in alphabetical order. She tried it—her mind raced through the names she could recall beginning with the letter A. Nothing rang a bell. She moved on to the B's. Barry, Bobby, Brent, Bubba. She laughed at that one. Imagine the Winslows knowing someone named Bubba. The list continued: Billy, Benjamin—Benjamin she repeated the name to herself—not quite. Benny, that's it. Bella said 'Benny'. Now to find—who is 'Benny'?

She remembered her mother's photo album. She and Ash had brought her luggage here to the condominium. Her photo album was in the suitcase. She returned to the bedroom, brought out the suitcase, opened it, retrieved the album, and began turning the pages. The pages were black paper with triangular corners holding the photos in place.

The pictures in the first pages seemed to be of her mother's high school days. There were group pictures that Scarlet assumed to be her mother's high school friends.

There were also individual photos of young men and women posing for their yearbook photos. The young men were in tuxedos and ties. The young women wore black velvet shoulder drapes with a single strand of pearls fastened at the neckline—furnished by the photographer. Scarlet remembered how she and her own friends had traded yearbook pictures.

Toward the final pages in the album, there were pictures of Jim O'Hara as a young man. He was handsome. The two made an attractive couple. He must have arrived in her mother's life after high school. She had always known that Marjorie and Jim were in love and that they both loved her.

Finally, she turned to the pages that held the pictures that had started this journey of discovery. There were several pages of pictures of the car—the Buick Park Avenue. Those old cars are big, she thought.

She continued turning the pages until the ones she was searching for showed up. There were several pictures of the Buick with different people posing beside it. There were two pictures of Doc Hadley. She did not recognize the others.

Taking a closer look she discovered an image that she thought could be of her dad, Jim O'Hara. He was standing alongside Doc Hadley in one of the photos. One of the men in the pictures is 'Benny'. She wondered how Bella knew him. He was probably a friend of her Papa. Somewhere in this album is a clue. Ash is right, I have to talk with my dad.

Chapter 39

She hurriedly gathered up her clothing and packed everything into the suitcase and the eco- friendly bags. She put on her jeans and a clean white shirt and called Ash on his cell phone. She asked if he could come home at lunchtime for a salad and sandwich. He replied that he could. She prepared the food, made lemonade, and waited for his arrival. He arrived at fifteen minutes past twelve.

While they ate lunch, she told him her plan.

"After looking at the photos I've decided you are right. I do need to talk to Dad. I got out the album and took a closer look at the pictures—the ones made of the Buick. I recognized one of the men as my dad, Jim O'Hara. He was much younger then and if my hunch is right, he was about thirty years younger. I need to talk to him. He must know more about my birth father than he has ever told me. This has become something I must do, even though I don't want to hurt Dad."

"I'd like to go with you and I can if you wait a few days. I'm busy with my own family right now. I need to do something about Mother. I didn't realize how she has failed until we spent some time with her. I suppose she was better at coping at her own home and found it difficult away from her surroundings. I have an idea that I think will be a good solution."

He paused and added, "Do you remember Dinah?—from Minnie's restaurant? I'm thinking I might ask her about quitting the restaurant and moving in with my mother. She lives in a little one room in the attic of Ollie Olsen's house. I think it would be a good thing for her and for Mother. I plan to check with her today."

"That sounds good. I expect Dinah has reached the age that waiting tables is getting more difficult. It will probably be good for both of them." Scarlet replied.

"Ash," she continued, "I appreciate your offer to go with me if I wait a few days, but I feel I need to go now. I've already packed a bag. I'm leaving some of my things here, if that's all right. I'd like to stay overnight at Dad's. There's a train out in about an hour. I made a reservation using my credit card. If it's all right with you, I would like to go to Richmond. I need to check on things there—see how my assistant is doing. I would pick up my car and drive back here."

"Of course, whatever works for you. I understand your need to go on right away. If that's your decision, I'll take you to the train. Let me say this, I'll count the days until you come back."

He took her in his arms and held her. It was as if he could not let her go. He kissed her—long, hungry kisses. When he released her, they kissed for a final time and left in the Hummer for the ride to the train station.

Chapter 40

Ash saw her off on the Carolinian and drove out to Minnie's for a cup of coffee and a serving of her peach cobbler with a huge dollop of ice cream.

When he finished eating, he called to Dinah, "Could I have a word with you, Dinah?"

"Any day, any time." She smiled as she sat down in the booth opposite him. "What's on your mind?"

Ash picked up a napkin, wiped the ice cream from around his mouth, and spoke, "Dinah, you've been working here as long as I can remember."

"Yeah, I been working here as long as I can remember," she replied, as she removed a cigarette from her pocket.

"Do you think you could give it all up?"

"What are you getting at? I can't work in that fancy pants restaurant of yours."

"Yes, you probably could, except I only have male waiters."

"How would I know? I ain't been in there yet. It's on my list of places to go before I die, though." Dinah was not usually so sarcastic.

He reached out to her and continued, "Dinah, I'd like to talk some business with you."

"What kind of business?"

"Come by after work and we'll talk. What time do you get

off?"

"Sometime around three this afternoon."

"Could you come by my office?"

"Yeah, I guess I could. You've got my curiosity up now."

"Good, I'll see you at three."

sh waited for Dinah to appear. He saw her old Dodge enter the parking lot and pull into a space. He watched as Dinah stepped out. She threw a cigarette in the grass and ground it out with the toe of her shoe, before entering the building. Ash thought they would have to reach a compromise on the cigarette business. He knew his mother wouldn't approve, or allow, smoking in her house.

Marlene showed Dinah into Ash's office. He pulled a chair up, facing his desk, and held it for her. She seemed uncomfortable in these surroundings.

He returned to the chair behind the desk and opened the conversation, "Dinah, how long have you been at Minnie's?"

"I don't know exactly. The boys were little tots when I went to work there. Maybe twelve or fifteen years."

"Do you make pretty good money?"

"If everyone was as generous with tips as Ashley Wilkes, I could say yes. It doesn't work that way, especially now with the hard times. Why do you ask me that? You do my taxes."

"As I said, I have an offer for you."

He leaned toward her across the desk and continued, "My mother is getting on up in years. I'm afraid she has reached the point where she needs someone to stay with her. I don't mean a cook or housekeeper. You would be more of a companion. Someone who could also help with the housekeeping and cooking. You know my mother will do her own work as long as she can, but she needs someone to help her. You could live there. It would be your home. Does that sound interesting?"

"I never thought about anything like that. A companion, you say?"

"Yes, that would be it, definitely not a hired hand. It would be your home and you would share the housekeeping with Mother. That is, if she will let you share the housework."

"Ash, I'm going to consider your offer. When do you need my answer?"

"As soon as possible. Just let me know in a day or two. Here is a figure I had in mind. I could pay you weekly or monthly."

He handed her a slip of paper with two figures, one a weekly amount and the other a monthly amount, written on it. When she saw the figures, she could have given her answer then, but she chose to make him wait a day or two—as if she were deciding. If she turned down that offer, folks would say she had lost her mind.

Chapter 42

The Carolinian arrived on time in Carrollton where Jim O'Hara waited for his daughter to step out of the passenger car. He saw her immediately and hurried to wrap her in a big bear hug. He loved this child. To Jim she would always be a child. She was even more precious to him since he lost her mother. He was hopeful that she would move back home. Carrollton finally had a mall and there were enough stores to keep her employed in her window decorating business.

He remembered how she had always been interested in fashions and decorating. All that stuff that looked so useless to him. He couldn't understand why the stores would go to all that expense to decorate a store window inside a mall. Folks rush by so fast they never take time to look.

He remembered how he and Marjorie used to go to the movies. After the movie, they enjoyed a walk through the downtown area. Marjorie enjoyed seeing the fashions displayed in the store windows and he observed the lighting, decor, and general theme. He wondered if she realized that most of the gifts he bought her came from the ideas he got from her comments as they stood outside on the sidewalk looking in at the models, wearing the latest fashions.

Scarlet was happy to see him. At that moment, she knew he would always be her dad. They went straight to his Honda CR-V and drove the short distance to the house that had always been her home. He had prepared a nice meal. They shared the chore of loading the dishwasher when they finished eating.

When they were finished in the kitchen, they moved into the comfortable den and sat in leather-upholstered chairs that faced the wide screen television set.

Scarlet was the first to speak, "How's it going, Dad. I know you're lonely with Mom gone."

"You can't imagine."

"I've had quite an adventure since I left here, a week or so ago."

"Adventure? Tell me about it."

"I've met someone."

"Yeah? I really want to hear this," Jim said.

"You won't believe it—his name is Ashley—Ashley Wilkes."

"Ashley Wilkes? You're right—I don't believe it, but your mother would love it!"

"It's true, Dad. He really is Ashley Wilkes. And—I'm growing fond of him."

"Fond?" Jim asked with a smile.

"Maybe more than fond."

"It happened so fast—you've only been gone a short time. Are you sure?" Jim inquired.

"We won't rush into anything. I wanted you to know."

"How did you meet him?"

She briefly related the story of meeting Ash in the McDonalds and the dinner at his restaurant.

"I thought the dinner would be the last I would see of him, but fate intervened." She paused before adding, "I was hit by a car and taken by ambulance to the hospital."

"Hit by a car—taken to the hospital. And, you didn't call me?" Jim interrupted.

"Oh, it wasn't anything. I had a bump on the head. They kept me overnight in the hospital. I had them call Ash and he came right away. Dad, he is so special." She paused and added, "It appears as if we were fated to meet. All of this happened in Royal, North Carolina."

"Royal?" he inquired.

"Yes, Dad, I've been to Royal."

"I wondered where you went when you left here that day on the train. I didn't think you were going to Richmond. I pretty much know the schedule of the Carolinian. Would you like to tell me about it?"

"It started with a photograph I found in Mom's old photo album."

"Yeah? A photo album. Must have been that old one that was up in the attic. I think those pictures went back to your mother's high school days."

"Yes, some of them did. The interesting ones were more recent. Maybe 29 or 30 years ago." Was it her imagination or did he perk up at that remark? He didn't say anything so she continued, "The ones I'm thinking of are pictures of a 1980 Buick. There are several folks posing with it. Do you remember?"

"Oh, God, yes, I remember. We need to talk."

"Can you tell me about Doc Hadley and someone named Benny?" she asked.

"I'll do my best. What do you want to know?" he replied.

"I want to know everything."

Jim sat quietly for a moment or two before beginning.

"This is a story we should have told you long ago. We always intended to tell you, but as time passed, we simply pushed it into the background. You know, of course that I am not your father, your birth father?"

"Yes, of course."

Jim leaned forward in the chair, looked at the floor, dropped his hands between his knees, and sat quietly for a short time. He began speaking, "Your mother and I desperately wanted a family. Time passed and it didn't happen. The doctors checked us both out. They told us that it was unlikely that we would ever conceive. My cousin, Doc Hadley—"

Scarlet interrupted, "Doc Hadley is your cousin?"

"Yes, a distant cousin. I think they call it third cousin. He and Benny Carlton came over here one Sunday afternoon."

"Benny Carlton?" she interrupted again.

"Yes, he was a friend of Doc's. I think that was the only time Doc ever came here. At the time, I wondered why he came. Benny had this new Buick Park Avenue and they were just riding around showing it off. We made pictures—lots of people stopped by to look at the car and get in the pictures.

"Doc started talking to me about being childless. Said one of the cousins had told him that we really wanted a baby. He told me about a baby due in about two months. The baby would be available for adoption. He assured us that it would be legal and he would take care of all the paper work. Your mother and I talked it over, prayed about it, and decided we wanted that baby.

"When you were born, a guy in a limousine and a nurse brought you here to the hospital. You were only a few hours old. You had to stay in an incubator at the hospital. Your mother and I spent all of our time at the hospital until we could bring you home with us."

"Dad, what are you saying? Mother is not my mother?"

"Oh Lord, honey, I'm so sorry. We should have told you from the beginning. Neither your mother nor I are your real parents. We meant to tell you. As time went on, it just didn't seem to be important. We loved you so much. You were newborn when we got you. Only hours old. It was entirely legal. Doc saw to that."

Scarlet began crying, "I can't believe it. I have always known that you were not my father, but now you tell me my mother is not my mother. This sounds like some cruel joke. I really am a giveaway."

Jim attempted to put his arms around her, but she pushed

him away.

"Dad, you said a man in a limousine brought me here. Do you know his name?"

"Let me think a minute. It was a long time ago," Jim said.

"Was the name—could it have been—was it Miles?"

"Miles—yes that was his name. They said he was British. He acted strange. He was very sad. We didn't get any details on the birth parents. We were just happy to get you and let Doc take care of all the details. They told us that the mother was from a prominent family and the father was a racecar driver. That's all we ever knew. Except we knew the racecar driver wanted a pay off and got a Buick Park Avenue car. Doc came here in that car—he and this Benny guy."

"Do you know who the parents were?" Scarlet asked.

"Nobody ever told us, but we always thought the father was Benny Carlton. Doc said the Buick was a payoff to the real father and Benny had a brand new Buick. Doc said the baby was Benny's, but Benny denied it. We never knew who the mother was. That was in the agreement." Jim continued, "We meant to tell you. Time passed and I guess we didn't have the heart to tell you after such a long time. I hope you can forgive us. Your mother and I—we wanted a baby and it took forever if you went through regular channels."

"What can you tell me about Benny Carlton?"

"Not much. I never saw him after the day he came with Doc. He seemed like an all right guy. We didn't talk much, but he did say he drove in some of the races. He was not big time, just local stuff."

"Do you think I—" she paused and continued, "you know, look like him?"

"He had bright red hair. No, I wouldn't say you favor him."

"I guess I must look like my mother, whoever she is. Will I ever know anything about my parents? Maybe DNA testing. I'll have to think about that." She sat quietly for a few minutes before continuing, "Dad, your cousin, Doc—he must have planned the whole thing to give me a good home."

"Whether he did or didn't, I can't say. One thing I can tell you, Scarlet—I couldn't love you anymore if you were my biological child. Your mother felt the same way. I know this is a shock and I'm sorry we didn't tell you the whole story. Can you forgive me—us?"

"Of course, Dad, it's just such a shock. I have to think about it. How could I not forgive you? You're the greatest dad in the world. "

"I love you, Scarlet. I have since the first moment I saw you in that incubator at the hospital. We received a call—I suppose it was from the British guy that brought you over here. We went directly to the hospital and met him there. The day we brought you home was one of the happiest days of my life."

Chapter 43

*S*carlet stayed overnight with Jim and left the following afternoon on the Carolinian, headed for Richmond. This was a good thing—she needed time to think. Her heart told her she had fallen in love with Ashley Wilkes. She believed that he had fallen in love with her. On the other hand, her head told her to slow down, take it easy. She hasn't known him long enough to be in love with him. Give it a little time.

At this point her plans are to confront Doc Hadley, Miles and the Winslow sisters. Doc Hadley was the contact to the prospective parents. If Miles delivered her to Mother and Dad, he must know something. If Miles was involved, the Winslow sisters are also involved.

After that, she would begin to think about Ash. She smiled. 'I won't worry about that today—I'll worry about that tomorrow.' The words of Miss Margaret Mitchell through the voice of Miss Scarlet O'Hara rang true to her today.

The train arrived on time. She went straight to her apartment. She had been gone three weeks. She inspected the plants first—they were in need of water. The water would revive them. They appeared to be in good condition only needing a small amount of snipping dead ends, in addition to the water—next the refrigerator. There was some spoilage. When the call came that her mother had died, she left immediately. She did not consider the contents of the refrigerator—big mistake. Sour milk—not a good thing!

Next, she tackled the mail. It's amazing how much can accumulate in a short time. So much junk. Then the e-mail. She went to the computer, logged in and was astonished at the amount of new mail. That's something else for another day—she could take care of that on Ash's computer when she returned to Royal.

She telephoned Mary Lynne, her assistant in the window dressing business and found that everything ran smoothly without her. Was that a good thing? She wasn't sure. Mary Lynne told her she could handle it for another ten days or two weeks.

"I'll be back long before then," she replied. She planned to get a good night's sleep. Tomorrow she would return to Royal. She could hardly wait to see Ash. It seemed that she had been gone much longer than overnight.

Rest was not to be hers yet. She opened the mail. There were bills to pay, and checks to deposit. Each storeowner paid her directly for her work. She had also done some freelance consulting in design for clients away from the mall. This business venture was very successful.

She wondered if she could realize the same amount of success in a town as small as Royal. She had the feeling that this would be a major concern for her in the very near future.

Chapter 44

$\mathcal{A}$sh had not seen or heard from Francine since the afternoon in the restaurant. He had not called her, nor had she called him. Sometime back, before he met Scarlet, he had begun to realize that their relationship was strictly for convenience. He was too involved to make changes.

At that time, he did not realize that they were habits to each other. Now he did not know what to do. No matter what the future held with Scarlet, he did not wish to continue with Francine, especially, after this latest news of the incidents with Marlene.

The best thing I can do is give her the opportunity to break off our relationship. Mother would say that is the proper thing to do. He speed dialed Francine's number and received her voice mail.

His message was brief and to the point. "Francine, this is Ash. We need to talk. Please give me a call." He hoped she would not call as he replaced the cell phone.

He left the office for the day, and headed to his restaurant. He had decided on a name—Ashley's Fine Dining.

He arrived at the restaurant just before the six o'clock opening time. He went straight to the kitchen where he made himself a salad and asked the chef to grill him a small rib eye. He speared a baked potato from the oven. He took it and the salad to the dining room. He ate the salad while waiting for the steak. Soon his rib eye arrived. He ate it and half of the baked potato.

He was well pleased with the restaurant. The manager was skilled at his job and had returned a fair profit each month, so far.

When the doors opened, several diners came in, were greeted by the hostess, and seated. Ash quietly observed as the restaurant filled up. He was very pleased. When he finished eating, he went around the tables. He greeted the diners and thanked them for coming. He went back into the kitchen, observed how smoothly everything ran, and was pleased. He left after quietly praising the staff.

As he drove into the underground garage at The Old School House, he realized that he had been reluctant to come home and not have Scarlet there to greet him.

Chapter 45

Scarlet arose early and used the ATM to leave her deposits, and to withdraw funds to last the next few days. She was on the road by eight in the morning. It was good to be on her way back to Royal.

She could hardly wait to see Ash. She looked at her watch and decided that she would surprise him at the office. When she drew near Royal, she saw a McDonalds sign looming in the distance. It was the restaurant where she had met Ashley. She decided to stop. She left the interstate at the next exit and parked near the entrance. She took some change from her purse, got out of the car, locked the doors, and entered McDonalds.

At the counter, she ordered a regular coffee with cream and sugar. She carried the coffee to a table by the window and sat down. The coffee was hot. She sat back to let it cool and looked around at the few customers. There was Doc Hadley—what to do? He apparently had not seen her. She couldn't decide whether to speak or leave without acknowledging him.

After a few minutes, she picked up the coffee and walked over to his table.

She spoke, "Hello, Doc. Remember me? Scarlet?"

"Oh, yes, I remember you. Have a seat."

She sat down opposite him and said, "Beautiful day, isn't it?"

"Yeah, I guess." He looked outside as if to check on the weather.

"I've just been to Carrollton. Had a talk with my dad, Jim O'Hara."

"How's Jim?" He did not attempt to deny knowing Jim O'Hara.

"He's fine. Did you know my mother passed away?"

"No, I didn't know that. I'm sorry to hear it. She was a good woman. Just in the last day or so?"

"Actually it was almost a month ago. I went to talk to Dad."

"How's Jim?" he asked again and went on, "I know he misses Marjorie. I remember how it was when my wife died."

"Yes, he does miss her but, he's doing well, all things considered."

She sat quietly for a few minutes and then said, "I had an interesting talk with Dad. He enlightened me about my real parents—I think he did. He said my father is a man called Benny Carlton. Dad also told me that you are his cousin. What do you think about that?"

"Third cousin isn't close kin. I've only seen him once since we grew up. Maybe once when we were kids. I think it was at a family reunion and my mama made me go."

"Doc, is Benny Carlton my father?" She looked him straight in the eye.

"That was the general consensus of opinion. Maybe nobody knows for sure. I sure as heck don't know. I knew of a baby that was due. One of my other cousins mentioned that your parents were looking to adopt. As far as I can see, I was doing a favor or two. I took care of the arrangements. Made everything nice and legal. It wasn't my business to find out who the baby's father was. I received a phone call when the baby was on its way. I gave information on the phone where to take the baby and that's all I know."

"What about a birth certificate?"

"The hospital took care of that."

"Then I suppose there is a record of my birth

somewhere?"

"I suppose so. Like I said—I just arranged the adoption."

"Where was I born?"

"I can't say." He was becoming impatient.

Scarlet picked up her cup of warm coffee, took a sip, and said, "I'm going to see Ash at his office. Have a nice day."

She walked to the car, turned and looked back at Doc, still sitting at the table. She got in the car and headed toward Ash's office.

Chapter 46

Scarlet drove on into Royal and headed for Ash's office in downtown. She parked behind the building and walked around to the front door. Marlene was not at her desk. Scarlet looked around and found Ash's office, tapped on the door, and smiled when he looked up and saw her standing in the hallway.

He came to the door, pulled her into the office, and held her in his arms. "I didn't know it was possible to miss someone as much as I missed you. Come in. Tell me about your trip." He pointed to a chair and pulled another one up beside her as she sat down. He closed the door and seated himself.

"It's good to be back. I missed you, too."

"Tell me about your trip. Did you learn anything?"

"More than I needed to know. The woman who raised me, the one I have called Mother all of my life? She's not my mother." She began to sob.

"Not your mother? Oh, Scarlet, baby." He dropped to his knees and put his arms around her. He stood again and lifted her up out of the chair, sat down in the chair himself, and held her.

After Scarlet calmed down, she briefly told him what she had learned from Jim.

He listened and when she finished he said, "What a shock! I can't imagine what you must feel."

"I feel so betrayed. All these years, I wasn't who I thought I was."

"No, you are the same person now that you were a week ago. Remember that. We'll get to the bottom of this, I promise."

"Have you had lunch?" he asked.

"No, I had a coffee at the McDonalds where we met. Oh, and guess who was there?"

"I have no idea," he replied.

"Doc Hadley. Next thing I know he'll be haunting my dreams."

"What did he have to say?" Ash asked.

"Not much. He apparently handled my adoption. He assured me that everything was legal and above board. They all think that a man named Benny Carlton is my father." Scarlet said.

"Where do we go from here?" Scarlet added.

"To the first floor of The Old School House," he replied.

"Yes, I suppose you're right."

Chapter 47

Ash and Scarlet left the office and headed toward the condominium, Ash in the Hummer leading the way. As prearranged, he drove into the garage and Scarlet parked in the front parking lot. They met at the entrance to Ash's unit. Ash unlocked the door, held it open for Scarlet, and followed her in.

"Sit down, Scarlet. I'll get you a glass of wine. It might help," Ash offered.

"Thank you," Scarlet replied.

He appeared in a short time with two glasses of wine and joined her in the den.

"What can I do?" he asked.

"I don't know," she replied.

"If Miles took you to the O'Haras, he must know the whole story. If he is involved, I'm sure the Winslow sisters are also involved."

"Yes, I suppose I must confront them. Is that the only alternative?"

"It's the only way you will learn the truth about your birth—your parents. I believe we need to pay them a visit. I'll go with you."

"All right, let's go. Should we call first?"

"I think we will just go and knock on the door, unannounced."

"I agree," Scarlet said.

They immediately descended to the first floor and rang the bell at number 101.

Miles came to the door and ushered them in.

"I will tell Miss Angela you are here. Please have a seat," he said.

They sat on the small sofa and waited for Angela, accompanied by Bella. Angela was distraught. She looked Scarlet straight in the eye and said, "How may I help you?"

Scarlet took a deep breath and said, "The pictures. I need an explanation. Is my father in that picture? I also need to know if Marjorie O'Hara is not my mother, who is my mother?"

Chapter 48

Angela walked across the Persian rug to the fireplace, placed her hand on the mantel, stood quite still for a moment, and turned to face the others in the room. She looked particularly at Scarlet and spoke, "Are your parents Jim and Marjorie O'Hara?"

"I grew up believing that Jim O'Hara was my stepfather and Marjorie O'Hara my mother."

"The time has come that I must reveal a secret that has been in this family for many years. Miles, will you please take Bella to her room."

"No, I believe Miss Bella needs to hear this, as well." Miles spoke with so much authority that everyone in the room drew a breath.

Angela could hardly believe her ears. Miles had defied her. What now? She stood in shock until she gained control enough to say, "Please, Miles. I beg of you." Miles did not move.

Bella did not appear to know what was taking place as Angela began speaking, "It all happened so long ago that it seems as though it were a dream. Bella and I led very sheltered lives. Mother saw to that. As we passed into our teenage years, we became somewhat more unwilling to obey her strict rules. I suppose that is natural. We made our debuts at the annual Terpsichorean Ball. We chose to debut into society at the same time, even though I am older."

Angela continued. "The results were not what Mother expected. She wanted the young men of the county to begin calling on us, but it did not happen. We did not know many of the townspeople—our lives were extremely sheltered. Papa hired a tutor to school us at home. Our escorts for the ball were the sons of the families here that owed Papa favors for one thing or another. None of this bothered me. You see, the marriage between my parents was not what I wanted from marriage. It was my only model. I assumed all marriages were like that. So years before, I had vowed that I would never marry. I did not wish to live apart from my husband, as my parents had done. Bella did not agree with my evaluation of the marriage situation."

Hesitantly she continued, "You have probably noticed that Bella is special. Mother always called it nervous and the doctors have other names for her condition. None of them seems to suit. When Miles came to us, one of his duties was to care for Bella. He was to look after her.

"At the debutante ball, Bella and I got our first taste of the male/female relationship. While it did not appeal to me, Bella was very enthusiastic. It was not too long after the ball that Papa brought a young man down from the mountain when he came for a visit. Bella immediately took a liking to him and they began to spend time together. When Papa realized this he took the young man back to the mountains, but the young man began to write Bella letters. She wrote him in return.

"We discovered sometime later that this young man, his name was Benny Carlton, had returned to Royal on several occasions and had been in the habit of coming to visit Bella in the afternoons. She would go for a walk and be gone a considerable amount of time. Mother had one of the maids follow her one afternoon. The maid reported that Bella had met Benny Carlton in a nearby park and got into his car.

"Mother summoned Papa back to town. He and Benny went into Papa's office and he persuaded young Benny Carlton to stay away from Bella. We heard quite a ruckus during this persuasion. Papa gave the young man a Buick automobile. I believe it is known as a Park Avenue."

Angela began to sob at this point and sat down. Bella also began to cry. Miles stood up, went to Bella, and led her from the room. She went willingly.

In a short while, Angela resumed speaking, "Bella was such an innocent. She was a dear child, but, in the body of a woman. Benny Carlton took advantage of her. I suppose you know what the outcome of that was?" No one spoke. Angela sat quietly to regain her composure. The door opened and closed as Miles returned to the drawing room.

Finally, Angela began speaking again, "Miles and I took Bella on an extended trip to the Eastern Shore for the final months of her confinement. We don't believe that Bella ever knew about the child. She was in such a state of mind that we were able to convince her she was gaining weight. When the time came for the arrival of the baby, we took her to a hospital. The baby arrived by Caesarean section. A family friend arranged all of this. I realize that all of this sounds impossible. You must remember the emotional condition of this young girl."

She looked at Scarlet and said, "I believe there is a possibility that you were that baby."

Scarlet began to weep. Ash turned toward her and placed his arms around her. He sat holding her. There was not a sound in the room except her weeping.

"So, this Benny Carlton—what happened to him? Is he living? My father," Scarlet asked through her tears.

"Papa put the fear of the Lord in him. He protested his innocence and disappeared. We heard that he raced in some of the small town races—nothing like NASCAR. When that was over, Papa never heard from him again, as far as I know. I understand there are ways to trace and find information on the internet."

"Yes, maybe I'll do that." Scarlet looked at Ash. She couldn't read his expression.

Miles walked to Scarlet, who was still sitting on the small sofa. He sighed, heavily and said, "They have it all wrong, Scarlet. Your search is over. I am your father." There was a universal gasp followed by complete silence.

Scarlet stared in disbelief. "But, how? I don't understand. I thought Benny Carlton—you know. I thought he was my father. Whoever Benny Carlton is."

Miles sat down in one of the comfortable chairs and began his story.

"Everything that was said about Benny Carlton was true, with one exception. You see, I followed Miss Bella on those walks and yes, she did get into the car with Benny, on several occasions. There was nothing inappropriate. I stayed nearby and they were never out of my sight. I tell you there was no sexual activity other than some heavy petting, as it was once called."

Angela had recovered her composure enough to ask a question. "Miles, in all these years I had no idea that you—that you and Bella—" her voice trailed off. She couldn't say it.

Miles continued, "I have loved Miss Bella as long as I can remember. Miss Bella gave me the nickname of Miles. Do you remember that, Miss Angela?"

"I'm not sure. Refresh my memory."

"We were on a trip, you, Miss Bella, your mother and, of course, your chauffeur. Your Papa was in the mountains at that time and did not accompany us. We were on our way home from the seacoast. Miss Bella was about fourteen years old at the time—still very much a child. This was long before the arrival of Benny Carlton. Your mother called my name and asked how many more miles before we would be home. Miss Bella took up the word 'miles' and began a little chant—a song saying repeatedly miles and miles and miles. After that, she began calling me Miles and soon it became my name. I was already in love with her and delighted that she had made up a pet name for me."

He looked around the room and added, "I am much older than Miss Bella and I have kept my secret all these years. The only thing I can do for her now is to look after her. I think she may love me in some way."

"But Miles, this doesn't explain your statement that you are Scarlet's father." Angela showed the extent of her confusion as she spoke.

"The last time I followed Miss Bella, when she met Benny Carlton, she saw me as she got out of the car. She was flushed and in a highly excited state. She ran to me and put her arms around me. She called me Benny. We walked home and went into the greenhouse."

He paused to allow this statement to take effect, before continuing, "I'm certain that I was the first—and the last. It was very unusual that a pregnancy occurred from that one time, but I can assure you it did. I remained quiet and let the blame fall on Benny Carlton. I am thoroughly ashamed of my actions." He paused again.

"When the baby, you, Scarlet, was born I felt that I could not give up that tiny bundle of pink and white, but I had no choice. They blamed Benny Carlton. I did not have the courage to admit my guilt. You must remember I was, and always have been, a servant in this household. I hope everyone involved can forgive me. I have never forgiven myself, but I ask that you, Scarlet, can find it in your heart to forgive me." Miles removed a handkerchief from his pocket and dried the tears from his eyes.

"I have been told that Doc Hadley had a role in this. That he arranged for my adoption. Is that true?" Scarlet asked.

"Yes, he was distantly related to Jim O'Hara. Jim and his wife wanted a baby. Doc Hadley made all of the arrangements for the adoption. I can assure you that everything was legal and that the O'Haras wanted you. Mr. Winslow gave the Buick, the one in the pictures, to Benny Carlton, as a bribe to get rid of him and his attentions to Miss Bella. I overheard one of the conversations between Benny and Mr. Winslow. Benny protested his innocence and tried to refuse the car, but his pleas fell on deaf ears. He finally accepted the car. No one believed him other than the trusted family chauffeur."

"So, it's true. Neither of my parents is my real mother and father. I've been living a lie for thirty years. My mother—" She looked toward Miss Bella, who had reappeared in the doorway, and began to sob hysterically. Ash took her in his arms and held her while this news penetrated her mind. "Poor Miss Bella is my mother," she whispered.

Bella suddenly appeared in the drawing room and called out, "Did I hear someone talking about Benny Carlton? Where is he?" She clutched the pocketbook in her hand.

Angela rose to the occasion as she had so many times through the years. "Yes, dear. We were just talking about what a nice young man he is. Papa thought so much of him."

"I love Benny. I've been saving my money and I'll find him someday." She opened the pocketbook and showed the roll of money. She continued speaking, "Did Papa give him a car? I thought he did. Benny will come back for me. I have my suitcase all packed and ready to go—wherever he takes me."

Miles, dear Miles moved in and took her by the hand, and led her back to her room. She did not protest. She willingly went with him. Perhaps she really does love him.

After that, it seemed that everyone simply dissolved and suddenly the room was empty.

Chapter 49

Neither Ash nor Scarlet slept well that night. Scarlet tossed and turned all night. Ash also had trouble falling asleep. He finally slept, and when he awoke at five o'clock, she was not in bed. He found her standing on the balcony with a cup of coffee. She was gazing toward the sunrise.

"Good morning." He kissed her softly.

"I know I kept you awake. It's just that I don't know who I am. My mother will always be my mother. I can't believe it is Miss Bella. She is so odd. I don't think she knows yet that I'm her—I can't even say it." Ash drew her into his arms.

"I think I understand how you feel. Poor Miss Bella isn't even an adult. I don't believe she would understand if we told her that she's your mother. As for Miles, he's a gem. I can see how he couldn't speak up and claim you. He was a servant. They would have accused him of rape. There's no telling what they would have done to him. I feel the others did about the only thing they could do. Remember, they, all of them, assumed that it was Benny Carlton. I'm sure he protested, but nobody believed him. He just took the car and ran. I can't say I blame him, under the circumstances. After all he knew he wasn't the father."

"Who is Miles? What is his name? I still don't know who I am." She began to sob.

"Tell me who you have been all these years."

"I don't know."

"You are the same person you have always been. I've prepared Miles's income tax returns for several years. If it will help, his name is Reginald Shelton. He came here from England as a child. I don't know anything about his parents. He will tell you what you need to know. He's an honorable man. It seems he didn't exist until he became the chauffeur for the Winslow family."

Ash continued speaking, "You'll decide who you are. If the O'Haras legally adopted you then you are legally Scarlet O'Hara. I feel certain it was all done legally and there won't be a problem. You will be the one to decide about Miles and Bella. You will have to decide if you want them in your life or not. That's up to you."

They sat quietly for a time before going inside. Together they made an omelet for breakfast. Ash whipped the eggs while Scarlet chopped up peppers and tomatoes. Toast and coffee completed the meal. Ash realized that Scarlet barely knew what she was eating.

Chapter 50

fter Ash left for the office, Scarlet sat on the balcony. She had not slept well. She had promised him that she would return to bed, and try to sleep a few hours, even though she knew that would be impossible. How does one sleep when one's life has turned into a lie?

Her mother was gone. No person could ever take the place of the woman who had so lovingly raised her. There isn't room for another.

Jim O'Hara was the only father she had ever known. They loved each other and had a special father/daughter relationship. She didn't think anyone, especially a stranger, could replace Jim. Could she make room in her life for another father?

What did she think about Miles and Miss Bella? The idea was too new for her to make any decisions. Miss Bella could never know that she was Scarlet's mother. It would be too traumatic. How would Miles fit in? Jim would always be her dad.

She began to wonder about Benny Carlton, now that it was certain that he was not her father. He was the scapegoat in this drama. Suddenly she thought again of the pictures in her mother's album. She dragged the album out once again and began looking at the pictures. She looked at one of the group pictures. They were all men. She could recognize Jim and Doc, but there were several more men in the pictures. Surely, one of them could be Benny Carlton.

She laid the album aside and crossed the room to Ash's desk. She turned on the computer and went on line. Google. com gave her several links to Benjamin (Benny) Carlton. She clicked on the first one. It read: Automobile dealership in the name of Carlton Motors. Successful businessman following a brief career in the racing arena. Always loved Buicks. Collects vintage autos. The listing named a city on the coast of North Carolina.

Scarlet leaned back in the chair. It was almost a whisper, "I'm going to find him and tell him who I am. I want to tell him that I know the truth."

Chapter 51

She hurriedly packed a few items in her suitcase—put on her jeans and a clean white shirt and called Ash.

"Hello, my darling. What can I do for you this morning?"

"Ash, I've located Benny Carlton. I'm all packed and ready to go."

"Go? Where are you going?" He sounded alarmed.

"Benny! Benny Carlton. I've found him. I can't wait to give him the news."

"News?"

"Yes, the news that we know he isn't my father."

"Scarlet, do you think we might just call him?"

"No, no I have to tell him face to face. I'm all packed and ready to go. I'll be back tomorrow."

"I suppose I can't talk you out of it?"

"No, I'll be back tomorrow. I have to do this. He owns, can you believe it, a Buick dealership on the coast."

She added, "Oh, and Ash, I'll hang up my clothes when I get back. That shows you how much I love you."

Ash dropped the cell phone. He called her back immediately, but did not get an answer. She never had that cell phone turned on.

"She'll probably drive me crazy," he muttered under his breath, smiling broadly.

Chapter 52

As he drove into the underground garage at The Old School House Ash realized that he had been reluctant to come home and not have Scarlet there to greet him. He couldn't face that lonely place now so he stopped on the first floor to visit.

Miles answered his ring and showed him into the drawing room. "So good to see you, Mr. Ashley. Please have a seat. I'll tell the ladies you are here. We had an early dinner."

"Is everything all right with you and the ladies, Miles?"

"Quite, all right, sir."

"I'm happy for you. Have they adjusted to the news?"

"I believe so, sir. We are trying to go on as if nothing had happened."

"Yes, I suppose that's best. Scarlet left this afternoon. She's going to see Benny Carlton."

Miles did not change expression when he said, "Very good, sir."

"Miles, how do you do it?"

"Do what, sir?"

"Live with them all these years and never mention the past."

"In the beginning, it was very difficult, but as time passed it became easier and easier. It was so long ago. Sometimes, I think it didn't happen. If Miss Bella had been well, we might have married, and that might not have been a good thing. Gossips can be so cruel and Miss Bella was, and still is, very fragile. I have taken care of her most of her life. As for me, I am happy that I finally met my daughter. I hope we can become acquainted. Excuse me, sir. I will fetch the ladies."

Ash thought, stiff upper lip and all that.

Chapter 53

It was going to be a beautiful day. Scarlet looked forward to seeing the ocean again. She made only one rest stop and, following her directions from Automap.com, she arrived at Benny Carlton's dealership well before noon. She parked her Camry in the parking lot of the dealership and went into the showroom. A sales clerk immediately greeted her.

"I'd like to see Mr. Carlton."

"One moment, I'll get him for you."

She tried to picture what he would look like while she waited. She was surprised at the sight of a handsome man of about fifty-five. He was dressed in a well-tailored custom-made suit, wore an expensive watch and a large ring with a diamond in the center.

He approached, extended his hand and spoke, "I'm Ben Carlton. How may I help you?"

"I'm Scarlet O'Hara, Mr. Carlton. May we speak privately?"

"Is this a joke? You are joking, aren't you? Scarlet O'Hara!"

"No, that's my name. My father had a sense of humor and my mother loved *Gone With The Wind*. May we go where we can talk?"

"Yes, of course. My office is this way." He pointed down the hall and followed her as she made her way toward his private office. She sat in a large, comfortable chair. He pulled up its twin and sat facing her.

"And, what can I do for you?" he asked.

"I don't know how to start."

"The beginning is usually a good place." He smiled pleasantly, made a tent by placing his fingertips together, and leaned back comfortably.

"Yes, you're right about that. The beginning is in the little town of Royal, North Carolina. The characters include Richard (Doc) Hadley, Jim O'Hara, a family named Winslow, a man called Miles, and a Buick Park Avenue car," Scarlet replied.

"That sounds like people I knew one time. You mentioned Jim O'Hara. Is he the Jim O'Hara that works for the Postal Service?"

"Yes, that's the one. He's my adoptive father."

"Do I know you? Is there something you want?"

"Yes, Mr. Carlton, there is something I want. I want to clear up a mistake—a thirty year mistake." She waited while he thought about her statement. She continued, "I have just learned, two days ago, that Miles Shelton is my father. I'm the daughter of Miles Shelton and Isabella Winslow. I think you'll recognize them by those names?"

"Yes, it has been a long time. I'm confused. Give me some details."

"To make a long story short, you were accused of fathering a child that was actually fathered by Miles Shelton." She paused briefly before continuing, "I'm that child. I came here to clear your name."

Benny Carlton sat speechless for a moment. He reached across the massive desk, picked up a large glass paperweight, and began rubbing it between his fingers, obviously a gesture to play for time as he tried to reconcile what he had heard.

At last, he gained control and was able to say, "It was Miles, that old rascal. I never thought about it being Miles— I've always heard it's the quiet ones you have to watch. This is amazing. I've lived with that burden for thirty years. Not one person would believe me and now you come here, finally, with the truth. Who are you?"

"I told you. I'm the child you were wrongfully accused of fathering."

He began to weep. "I had thought that would haunt me to my grave. After all these years the truth is coming out." He removed a handkerchief from his pocket and wiped the tears from his eyes and face. She briefly told him her story.

"Scarlet, is that your real name?" She nodded yes and he continued, "I was a bit of a hell-raiser back in those days, but I didn't mess with that girl. I couldn't take advantage of someone like her. That girl, Bella. Arch told me about the ball that she and Miss Angela attended. He said she seemed to go crazy after that. She was a pretty, little thing. I guess the boys gave her a good time dancing with her.

"What I'm saying is—" he paused before continuing, "Arch wanted me to pay a little attention to her. He didn't want Mrs. Winslow or Miss Angela to know. He brought me down from the mountain and I spent some time with her. We met in the park a couple times. I swear I never touched her other than a few kisses in my old car. The last time I was with her that chauffeur, Miles, she called him, came to the car, and took her home. I left and went back to the mountains and never saw her again.

"A couple of months later her parents called me in and accused me of getting her pregnant. I denied it, but they wouldn't believe me. They offered me the Buick to shut me up. They wouldn't believe that I hadn't done it. Finally I took the Buick and left." He paused before adding, "How did this all come out in the open?"

Scarlet briefly explained how she learned about her birth and adoption.

"You know she wasn't right. Bella wasn't. They said she had a terrible fall when she was about eleven years old and was never right after that. Fell on the slate patio and hit her head.

Stayed unconscious for several hours. It messed her up good."

"Mr. Carlton—" she started.

"Please call me Ben. I cannot tell you how happy I am to hear this from you. The only way I got through it was I knew it was not true. My conscience was clear. My wife has never believed the stories. She's very special and has helped me to accept the gossip and rumors as just what they are."

Scarlet started again, "I want you to know that Miles has loved Bella since she was a teenager. It happened the afternoon when he took her from your car. It—" She paused, looked away, and continued, "It was just the one time."

Scarlet decided against telling Ben about Bella's obsession that he was coming back for her. What purpose would that serve?

"I understand you were a race car driver? That seems to have been a colorful time—the moonshine liquor, fast cars, and the law enforcement officers."

"That was before my time. My dad ran 'shine'. He was very good at eluding the law enforcement officers." He smiled at this and continued, "They were referred to as 'revenuers'."

"Yes, that must have been a very colorful time. I must leave now. I'm driving to Royal this afternoon and I'll stay there a few days before I return to Richmond. If you are ever in Richmond, feel free to contact me. I'm in the phone book."

She held her hand out and he clasped it with his large one and said, "Thank you for this gift."

She arose from the chair, walked to the credenza behind his desk, and asked, "May I?"

"Look at the pictures? Of course. That's my family. I have two daughters, two sons-in-law, and four grandchildren. I'm a lucky man!"

She started to the door, turned and added, "I may not remain in Richmond. I will probably relocate to Royal in the near future. Good-bye, Ben."

"Good bye, Scarlet O'Hara. It has been a real pleasure to

meet you. Come again. I appreciate what you have done for me. Thank you."

Scarlet left the parking lot aware that Benjamin Carlton stood behind the large plate glass window watching her departure. She looked at the clock on the dashboard and realized there was no reason for her to stay overnight. She could drive to Royal and arrive about the time that Ash would be getting home. She could hardly wait.

The drive was uneventful and she, as planned, arrived at Ash's condominium just ahead of him. She parked in front of the building. He saw her as he approached the driveway, turned into the parking lot, and jumped from the Hummer. He ran to her with arms opened wide. They met in the parking lot.

"Oh, how I missed you," he said.

"Yes me, too."

"Come inside. We've so much to talk about."

"You just don't know!"

Ash listened attentively as she told him about the drive to the coast and her visit with Benny Carlton.

"Ash, he was so different than I had pictured him. He's so nice and has a successful business, a wife, and family. He showed me pictures of his family, all lined up on a console behind his desk. I'd like to go back to see him sometime."

"Yes, of course we can. I love the coast. And, now, tell me about your business."

"Mary Lynne is doing the windows and I have a few more days off. I probably need to go back in a week."

"Great, I have so much to tell you. First, I have engaged Dinah, you remember from Minnie's, to move in and stay with Mother. It will be her home. She's thrilled finally to get away from that room in the attic at Ollie Olsen's. Miles is anxious to get to know you. He would like to spend some time with you. And, oh yes," he added as an afterthought, "I am out of a relationship that I—"

Scarlet interrupted, "Say no more." She began kissing

him.

"And, oh yes, about Richmond. I may look for clients in Royal. I've grown quite fond of this town."

"Sounds good to me."

Chapter 54

The telephone rang soon after Ash left for the office. Scarlet answered, "Good Morning."

"Good morning. Is this Scarlet?"

"Yes."

"This is Doc Hadley."

"Doc? I hope you're well." She could not think of anything to say to him.

"Yes, I'm fine. Could we talk?"

"Talk? About what?"

"I have some things I need to tell you."

"You were not interested in talking to me the last time I saw you."

"Sorry about that. Things have changed. Maybe, I changed. Anyway, I'd like to talk with you. How about the conference room at the library, it's usually available."

"I could meet you about one o'clock."

"Fine, I'll see you then. Oh, yeah, come alone."

"Doc, you sound sinister. Is this a joke?"

"No, I promise you it's no joke. And, it isn't sinister—just private."

"I'll see you at one."

Chapter 55

Scarlet called Ash and told him about the phone call from Doc.

"Do I need to go with you?" he asked.

"No, he specifically said to come alone."

"This does not sound good. It certainly does not sound like something Doc would do. I think I should go with you."

"Oh, Ash, I'm a big girl—besides Doc is harmless. Don't worry about it. I'll call you after I talk with him."

"Promise?"

"I promise."

She drove into the parking lot at the library just before one o'clock. She parked next to Doc's pickup truck and went in. He was waiting in the small conference room. He arose when she entered and closed the door. As soon as they sat down, he started, "Scarlet, I don't know where to begin."

"The beginning is usually a good place." She repeated the words that Benny Carlton had said to her.

"Miles told me you knew the whole story, but you don't actually. I'd like to tell my part in this."

"Go ahead."

"The beginning, or maybe it's the ending, is a resort community on the eastern shore of Maryland, to be exact. When Miss Angela discovered that Miss Bella was pregnant, she immediately called me. I've always been their family friend.

They, Miss Angela and Miss Bella, are helpless in matters of business. Things like getting electricity, telephone service. They did not have a clue. Arch Winslow depended on me to look after them. He spent most of his time in the mountains.

"We Arch and I carefully planned the next few months. As soon as the pregnancy became visible, I took the two sisters, Miss Angela and Miss Isabella to a coastal area in Maryland. I had made all of the arrangements. I leased a small house and took care of everything.

"I drove them to Maryland. At that time, we did not want anyone to know about the plans, not even Miles. We all naturally assumed that Benny was the father, because of Miss Bella's obsession with him.

"I left the two sisters there. It soon became apparent that Miss Angela could not manage the situation on her own. She called me and I sent the faithful servant, Miles to look after them. We made detailed plans for the following months. We followed these plans to the letter. When the time came for the C-section, I returned. Miss Angela and Miles had made all the arrangements for the birth and I had arranged for the adoption.

"Everything fell into place. The baby, a girl, was born." He looked at Scarlet and she nodded her head acknowledging that she understood. He was talking about her birth.

"As we had planned, as soon as you were born, Miles left, with a registered nurse in tow. Because you were so tiny, you went immediately to the hospital in Carrolton, Virginia. They placed you in an incubator. They had a private duty nurse there to take care of you. All of these plans, arranged in the weeks before your birth, worked out perfectly. No detail was overlooked." Doc paused in his story and began again, "Marjorie and Jim were at the hospital every day until they could take you home with them."

Doc realized that Scarlet had begun to weep. He paused in his story until, she said, "Go on."

"You were in the hospital until your weight gain was sufficient to allow home care. The nurse stayed with you for a day or two, after they took you home. I don't remember just how long, but she stayed until she felt comfortable leaving you."

He paused before continuing, "I took care of the birth certificate, everything. It was all properly taken care of."

"I appreciate your telling me all of this. It makes me feel better about—" She arose, anxious to leave.

Doc held up his hand and said, "Wait, there's more." She sat back down and waited for him to continue.

"There was another baby."

Chapter 56

Scarlet did not move. She couldn't speak. Doc continued, "While Miles went to Carrolton, I stayed at the hospital with Miss Angela. I was there when the doctor came out of the delivery room and told us there was another tiny baby—a boy. Miss Angela fainted. When we revived her, she had us call social services, and they took the boy. It was easy to find him a home. They placed him with a young couple.

"Miss Angela and I arranged for Miss Bella to go to a private facility to recuperate. Miss Bella stayed in some kind of sedation. She never realized what had happened. In addition to her emotional condition, she is very naïve and trusting. She trusted Miss Angela. Miss Angela stayed on in the cottage, with Miles to take care of her. When both of the sisters recuperated they returned to Royal."

"Did Miles know about the boy?"

"No. That happened while he was taking you to the O'Hara's house. As far as I know, Miles never knew about the boy. I'm pretty sure neither Miles nor Benny ever knew there was a second baby. Only Miss Angela and I knew about that. Except, of course, the hospital personnel and social services knew."

"Doc, I can't handle any more information now. I'll have to absorb what you've told me and we will talk again." She arose and started toward the door.

"Scarlet, forgive me. I thought I was doing the right thing.

Miss Angela pledged me to secrecy. Try to see my side of the story."

"I told you, I can't deal with it now. I'll talk to you later." She left the library and returned to Ash's condominium.

Chapter 57

*A*sh was in disbelief when she told him about the second baby. "Scarlet, this sounds like a fairy tale," he said.

"You have been a rock through all of this. I hope there are no more secrets surrounding my birth. I want to see about contacting this brother of mine. I had no idea I had any relatives. Can we look up birth records online?"

"I'm sure we can, but I think I would like for us to go to Maryland and search this out. I feel you might want to see the place where you were born. Perhaps, find the cottage where they lived. It would make it all seem more real to you. Would you like that?"

"Oh, yes. When can we leave?"

"We will need to be there on a week day to go to the courthouse or wherever the records are stored. We can go tomorrow. I'll make arrangements. We'll leave tomorrow morning. How does that sound?"

"It sounds good. I'm sorry to take you away from your office."

"That's OK. Marlene can handle most anything that comes up."

Ash continued, "Marlene is more than capable as my administrative assistant…"

Scarlet interrupted, "Administrative assistant? Have

you joined the twenty first century? What happened to secretary?"

"Yes, I'm trying to mend my ways. That's a start. We had our little chat—I told her I was disappointed she chose to interfere in my personal life, and her behavior was reprehensible. It took a few days, but she apologized profusely and promised her unflagging devotion from now on. We made peace and so far, she has kept her promise."

Chapter 58

Ash was true to his word. The following morning they were on their way to a small town on the coast of Maryland. The weather was beautiful. It could have been a delightful trip under different circumstances. Ash tried to cheer Scarlet and she tried very hard to cooperate. They stopped several times along the way to eat or just sightsee. Ash had said they would take one day for the drive to Maryland and tend to business the second day.

They arrived at the seacoast town at twilight and checked into their room. The balcony overlooked the Atlantic Ocean. After dinner in the hotel dining room, they walked the beach, hand in hand. Ash tried in every way possible to keep her mind off the situation. Finally, they went in and retired early.

After breakfast in the hotel dining room, they went to the county courthouse located inland a few miles. All they had was the date of birth and the fact that there were twins born. The clerk assisting them found the records of the birth immediately. Sure enough, there was the record in black and white. Two babies, one male, and one female born on May 23, 1980—the births took place twenty minutes apart.

Later in the day, Ash and Scarlet visited the hospital archives and discovered that the female baby went to another hospital. The male baby remained at this hospital in an incubator. Michael and Henrietta Stewart took the male baby to their home three weeks later.

Chapter 59

"None of this seems real. I could never have imagined this scenario," Scarlet said. They had returned to the hotel and begun to repack for the return to Royal.

"While you were napping, I found out where the cottage is that Angela and Isabella stayed in. Doc gave me the address and I looked it up. Would you like to see it?"

"No, I don't think so. But I would like to meet the Stewarts—do you think it would be all right if we called them?"

"I don't know why not. I have the number right here." He handed her a slip of paper. She went to the telephone and dialed the number. There was no answer.

Ash said, "I have the address. We'll drive out and at least see where they live."

The bellman took their two bags to the Hummer and they left the hotel. The town wasn't much more than a village. Ash had no trouble finding the house where the Stewarts lived. It was a nice brick bungalow about a block from the ocean. The colorful flowerbeds along the front of the house accented the freshly mowed lawn. An American flag was flying from the porch railing.

Ash pulled to the curb, turned the engine off, and turned to Scarlet. "It's a nice middle class home. I'm sure your brother has a good life." He reached for her hand, brought it to his lips, and kissed it.

A car appeared on the street and turned into the driveway as they looked on. Ash opened the car door and stepped out. The car stopped and the door opened. The driver got out and asked, "Something I can do for you?"

Ash walked toward him, held out his hand and said, "Mr. Stewart?"

"Yes, I'm Mike Stewart." He reached for the proffered hand.

"My name is Ashley Wilkes and this is Scarlet O'Hara." He pointed toward Scarlet as he spoke.

"You're kidding, aren't you?"

"I'm afraid not. That's a long story. Scarlet has something she wants to say to you."

Suddenly Scarlet was speechless. She began to weep and by this time, Mrs. Stewart had approached. She handed Scarlet a tissue and said, "Please come inside. Whatever is wrong, it can't be all that bad. Come with me."

The two couples entered the house. "We're Mike and Henrietta. How about a cup of coffee—or would you rather have iced tea?"

Ash answered, "Nothing, thank you."

Scarlet was getting control of herself by this time and spoke, "Mrs. Stewart, we came to see your son. I believe he's my brother. My twin brother."

Henrietta looked as if she would faint. Her husband went to her and helped her into a chair. The Stewarts did not know that their son was a twin. They seemed to be as shocked as Scarlet had been when she found out that she had a brother. "I'm anxious to meet him. Does he live with you?"

Henrietta began weeping again and Mike answered the question, "Our son was killed in the Gulf War." He pointed to the gold star in the front window.

"I'm so sorry." Scarlet was at a loss for words.

Mike continued, "He enlisted, completed basic training,

took some specialized training and went over to the gulf. They got him in about ten days—snipers." Mike broke down and cried. "He was all we had."

They sat quietly for a while. Henrietta asked, "You say you're his twin? We didn't know about you. We had applied for adoption and waited a couple of years when unexpectedly our doctor called and said we could have this baby boy if we could get him right away. He stayed in the hospital several weeks. We gave him a good home. He was a good boy—a good man."

"I'm so sorry. I just found out a few days ago that I had a twin. I'm sorry I didn't know before. What did you name him—my brother?"

"He was Trenton Alan Stewart. He was named after his two grandfathers and was called Trent." Henrietta paused before continuing, "What can you tell us about his birth?"

"As I said, I've just recently learned who my birth parents are. I'm still trying to deal with it. I wanted to meet my twin and see if we could work it out together. This is what I know..." Scarlet began briefly to tell the story to the Stewarts.

Ash sat beside her on the sofa as she talked. She was relieved of a burden with each word that she spoke. The Stewarts listened intently. Ash felt that he had witnessed a catharsis. This trip was a good thing.

"Ash, there's nothing like family, is there?" They were on the way back to Royal.

"You're right there."

"I want to visit Miles and include him in my life. Jim will always be my dad, though. I'll have to make room for two dads, I suppose."

"You can do that. You have a big heart."

"Thanks, you, too. Ash, I think I love you."

"I think you do, too." He smiled and put her hand to his lips. They would soon be home.

Chapter 60

They arrived back at Ash's, after stopping for dinner along the way. Ash realized that Scarlet was exhausted. The day had been the strangest of her life. She had lost a brother she never knew she had, and gained friends, Mike and Henrietta Stewart. He drew a hot bath for her and insisted that she soak some of the weariness away. He suggested that she go to bed and try to sleep.

After he tucked her in, Ash dialed the telephone number of his mother. Dinah had already moved in, but was working the usual two-week notice at Minnie's restaurant.

Annette answered the telephone, "Hello, Ash."

"Hello, Mother. I hope you and your new housemate are doing well."

"Oh, my, yes. Dinah is setting my hair. Wait until you see the color she put in. I'm positively gorgeous. Dinah said so."

"Dare I ask what color?"

"No, it's a surprise," Annette replied.

"Not too much of a surprise, I hope."

"It's little bit of a reddish brown. It may be auburn. I look ten years younger."

"Well, we could all use a little of that," Ash said.

"How's Charlotte?" she asked.

"She's fine," he said.

"Dinah just said her name is Scarlet. Is that right?"

"Yes, that's right, Mother."

"Then why didn't you say so? Gotta run. Thanks for calling."

Ashley's internal voice spoke, "What has Dinah done to my mother?"

Chapter 61

Scarlet saw Ash off to work the next morning and set about getting her clothes in order. She needed to go back to Richmond, but she wanted to talk to Miles before leaving. She called the number that Ash had jotted on the pad near the telephone.

Miles answered on the second ring, "Good morning. This is the Winslow residence, Miles speaking."

"Good morning, Miles. This is Scarlet. Could you come upstairs to Ash's? We need to talk," she requested.

He hesitated, before saying, "Yes, I will be right up."

When the bell chimed, Scarlet opened the door and invited him in.

It was a tense meeting until she greeted him warmly and said, "Please come in, Miles. Have a seat." She motioned toward the sofa.

"I will stand, if you don't mind." He was very uncomfortable.

"Please sit down. I have something to tell you." He hesitantly sat on the edge of the sofa.

"Miles, I don't know how to begin." She sat beside him on the sofa and reached for his hand.

She said, "I was a twin—you also had a son."

Miles paled and stammered, "A son? There was a son?"

She told him about the conversation with Doc and the trip

to Maryland. It was very difficult to give him the news that a son was born on that morning in May, so long ago. And, even more difficult to tell him that the son died as a hero in the Gulf War.

He received the news in typical British fashion. He sat quietly, there on the sofa, drew a linen handkerchief from his pocket and wiped the tears away. He sat quietly for a few minutes and arose to leave.

"I don't know what to say. I have held so much inside all of these years—since your birth—I'm at a loss as to what to say, or even to think."

"We will work it out together. You know, that Jim will always be my dad, but I will make room in my heart for you." She said as she wiped tears from her eyes.

"Miles," she began "I don't know what to call you."

"Just call me Miles. That will please me very much."

"Thank you, Miles. I don't know how to do this."

"Neither do I—I don't know what to call you. Should I call you Miss? Scarlet? What is appropriate?"

"I'm sure I don't know. How about Scarlet? Is that all right with you?"

"Yes, Miss. I mean, yes, Scarlet."

"Oh, Miles, you're just too British!"

"I believe you have hit it on the head, Miss."

"Miles, call me Scarlet."

"I'll try—Scarlet."

"Do we shake hands or hug?" she asked.

"I would like a hug, if you don't mind, Scarlet."

"I can do that," Scarlet replied with her arms held wide.

Miles said, "Some way, we will learn what our relation will be. It may take a while, but, we will do it."

Chapter 62

ater that evening Ash suggested, "We need to talk. Let's go to the den." Scarlet followed him. They sat on the sofa. Ash took her hand in his. He drew it to his lips and kissed it tenderly. He pulled her into the fold of his arms. She snuggled against his chest.

"Scarlet," he began, "I realize we haven't known each other very long. I'm not one to rush into anything, and yet, my heart tells me I love you. My head says wait, it's too soon." He kissed the top of her head.

"Which one do you listen to? Your heart or your head?" she asked.

"My heart, of course," he said.

"Then tell me. What's the problem? I love you, Ashley Wilkes."

He kissed her.

"And, I love you, Scarlet O'Hara." He kissed her again.

"We don't have to make any plans or decisions now. Just as long as we know how we feel. There's no rush." Ash continued, "So much has happened to us—especially to you. Perhaps we should continue as we are for awhile."

"Yes, I need to go home, to Richmond. I'm sure Mary Lynne is doing a good job, but it's my business and I've been away nearly a month. I thought I might leave over the weekend. I could leave Sunday and you might come to Richmond next weekend. I could show you around. It's a big city and we could have fun," she suggested.

"That sounds like an excellent, but temporary plan." He took her into his arms and kissed her.

For the next few weekends, they followed a schedule—Ash was in Richmond one weekend and Scarlet was in Royal the next weekend.

On the weekends that Ash was in Richmond, they had fun checking out the restaurants and comparing them with Ashley's Fine Dining. They saw plays, attended movies, and visited the museums of the city. Ash loved city life, but was happy to return to Royal.

The weekends in Royal were much quieter. Scarlet arrived on Friday. She spent the day calling on businesses at the Green Leaf Mall. Soon she had lined up clients in Royal and established a branch. Now she was the owner of two businesses. Mary Lynne managed the Richmond branch and Scarlet managed the new one.

Chapter 63

sh appeared to be anxious. Scarlet watched him pace around the condominium as she dressed for their evening out. He had asked her to dress up in something special. She had bought a dress in one of the high-end shops in Richmond. The new dress was a coral, satin sheath with a neckline cut very low in front. She had a necklace of coral stones, pearls, and sterling silver, with matching pendant earrings. Her hair was swept away from her face. She had her hair done in Richmond—manicure and pedicure, too. Ash had never seen her so dressed up.

The doorbell rang—he opened the door. A chauffeur in full uniform, cap in hand stood in the hallway.

"Your limousine is here, sir."

"One moment, please."

Ash turned to call for Scarlet and found her standing in the doorway to the foyer. She was so lovely he gasped.

"Ash, we have a limousine? Where are we going?"

"It's a surprise. No more questions."

He placed her wrap around her shoulders. They left the condominium and followed the chauffeur downstairs to the parking lot.

The chauffeur opened the door and stood at attention as they seated themselves in the rear seat. He closed the door and entered on the drivers' side, started the motor, and drove out of the parking lot.

"Ash, this is wonderful. You really know how to treat a girl." She leaned over and kissed him.

He removed a bottle of champagne from the bar, filled two glasses, and proposed a toast. He raised his glass and said, "To the loveliest lady of them all."

Scarlet didn't pay any attention to where they were going. The limousine stopped. The chauffeur hastily got out and opened the door. Ashley and Scarlet got out and when Scarlet looked around, she realized they were at Ashley's Fine Dining. The new sign was up and lighted. There were no cars in the parking lot. Ashley escorted her to the door, opened it and they entered.

The lights were burning low, soft music was playing, and candles were everywhere. The dining room was empty. They were the only occupants. Ashley guided her to a table set for two with lovely china and crystal. Scarlet was speechless as Ashley seated her. He sat facing her and lifted his glass in a toast, "To the love of my life."

One lone waiter served the meal in complete silence. After dessert, Ash led Scarlet to the patio and another blaze of candlelight. The music followed them. Once they were outside, as if on cue, the music stopped. He guided her to a wrought iron chair, seated her, and dropped to his knees.

"Scarlet, love of my life, my heart is yours. Will you do me the honor of becoming my wife?"

"Yes, oh yes." Her big blue eyes glistened with tears, "I thought you would never ask!" He placed the sparkling diamond ring on her finger and kissed her with tenderness.

Scarlet added, "Oh Ash, this is truly a happy ending. I started a search to find my real father and ended up finding the love of my life, too! I just can't believe it's real."

"Believe it," Ash replied, "this is the real storybook ending."

Chapter 64

On Christmas Eve, Scarlet stood in the narthex of the Methodist Church with her two dads, Miles and Jim, one on each side. The church glowed with candlelight and white poinsettias.

She was waiting for the cue that would start her journey down the aisle to the man of her dreams. It had been a wonderful year. Her life had taken a ninety-degree turn. She had found her birth parents and made new friends. Miles was happy to be part of her life. Isabella was pleased to become Auntie Bella. Angela had welcomed her into the family as her only niece. She had an entirely new family and new friends. Think about it—it all started at McDonalds.

Jim spoke first, "If only your mother could be here. How happy she would be!"

Miles interjected, "Her mother is here. Right down front, even though she has no memory of it. As for me, in a few minutes I will have given my daughter away two times."

Scarlet said, "I'm the luckiest girl in town. I've had two mothers and two fathers."

The two men shook hands, as the organist gave the cue for the first step. Scarlet smiled at Ash at the end of the aisle waiting so patiently for her. He smiled in return as she made the first step down the aisle to the love of her life.

Annette Wilkes, seated in the first pew, turned to Dinah and said, "Who is that girl in the long white dress?"